The Whistler

'Sooner or later, Tom, the Whistler will suggest that you do something shady. He may not see any harm in it, because that's the way he's always done things. Can you say 'no' when the time comes?'

Tom wasn't sure.

The Whistler

Veronica Heley

SCRIPTURE UNION
130 City Road, London EC1V 2NJ

By the same author:
Sparrow

© Veronica Heley 1985

First published 1985

ISBN 0 86201 312 7

Printed and bound in Great Britain by
Cox & Wyman Ltd, Reading

1

They were to be separated. Tom couldn't believe it. It simply could not be happening to them.

It was the twins' first day at Fairfield Comprehensive, and the new intake was being called out, form by form, to go off into the unknown depths of the school.

'Forrester, D. Follow Mr Budd. You're in class three.'

Tom's twin brother got up from among the crowd of new boys and girls waiting to be sent to their form rooms, and went out of the hall with twenty-odd other children.

Tom couldn't bear it. He jumped up, too. 'He's my brother. I must go with him.'

The teacher gave Tom a cross look. 'Sit down and wait till I call out your name.'

'But . . .'

'Sit!' The teacher might be a weed to look at, but she had the sort of voice you'd expect from a sergeant major.

Tom sat.

He muttered, 'Silly old cow.'

'What was that you said?' The teacher couldn't possibly have heard.

'Nothing,' said Tom.

'Nothing, miss,' said the teacher, exacting tribute.

'Nothing miss,' said Tom. 'But . . .'

'But . . . ?'

Everyone was looking at him, and he could feel his ears going red. Normally he'd have let it go, and argued later. But this was important.

'We're twins, miss. We've never been separated before. There must be some mistake.'

'What's your name?'

'Tom Forrester.'

The teacher checked her list. 'Forrester, T. You're in Mr Carton's form, class five. We don't believe in allowing twins to sit together in this school. That way, you develop your own personalities. Now if you will kindly allow me to proceed? We do have nearly a hundred more names to get through. We'll start a new line over by the door.'

The teacher ploughed on, reading out names, and Tom slumped, clutching his stomach. He felt sick. Perhaps he would be sick, really truly, there and then on the floor. That would serve them right. When he was little, he could make himself sick up anything, by putting a finger down his throat. It had been quite useful if he and Davy had wanted to get out of doing the chores about the house. Tom would make himself sick, and then Davy would talk them out of doing their homework, or mowing the lawn, or whatever.

Two great globs gathered in the corners of Tom's eyes, and he felt that if he weren't careful, he might be seen crying, on his first day in the new school. He'd never live that down, never.

He glanced to left and right of him, and saw that the others were looking at him with something like admiration. He'd been the only one to stand up to that weed of a teacher, and they'd remember that.

6

Tom felt a little better when he saw that they were looking at him with admiration. Almost, it made up for the miserable feeling inside him when he thought of Davy going off into their new school without him.

Davy might have said something, Tom thought. He hadn't even tried to argue. He'd gone off, as meek as a girl.

It was Tom's turn to be marched off to report to his new form master. Mr Carton was a middle-aged man with a permanently sniffy nose. He looked as if he'd spent all his life in front of a blackboard, with one eye out on a stalk at the top of his head ready to spot trouble before it got going.

Tom felt depressed, looking at Mr Carton. He was the spitting image of the chap they'd had for Maths at their last school, and the problems which Tom had had last year with his Maths were obviously going to come up all over again.

'Stinking school!' said Tom, more or less under his breath.

'Dead right!' said a sharp-looking, dark-haired lad on Tom's right.

'You, there,' said the form master. 'If you have anything to say, we'd all like to hear it.'

The lad with the sharp face got up, slowly, taking his time about it to show that no matter what the teacher said, he was not going to hurry himself.

'Yessir?'

'What's your name, boy?'

'The Whistler, sir.'

Mr Carton consulted a list. 'I don't see that name down here. Since this form is mostly composed of those boys and girls whose surnames begin with the initials G and H, I fear you must have joined us in error.'

'Sorry, sir,' said the Whistler. 'It's my nickname, you know.' And he whistled a snatch of tune so well that everyone turned round to look at him, with a smile.

'Oh, a nickname!' Mr Carton was not amused. 'Well, perhaps you'd be so good as to favour us with your real name, so that I can mark your card accordingly.'

'Gardam, sir,' said the Whistler, with a wink at Tom.

Everyone who'd seen the wink, now laughed aloud.

'Stop that!' said Mr Carton, blowing his nose with relish. They stopped. This was a brand new world, and they weren't yet sure of their place in it. It was time to tread softly.

'Now,' said Mr Carton, 'You will all come here first thing every morning, in period one, for registration. The rest of the day you will spend going from one part of the school to another. You will go for science lessons to the Science block, and for woodwork to the Art department. I will give you maps and timetables so that you can work out where you should be at any given time. This morning you will have tests for English, Maths and French, so that we can separate you into groups, or sets. Those who have a good grasp of the subject will go into a higher group, those who need a lot of help will get it, lower down. All the rest of your classes will be mixed ability, and you will go to them as a form, together. Now, are there any questions?'

'Please, sir,' said Tom.

'What's your name?'

'Forrester, sir.'

'I shouldn't have any Fs in my class. Are you sure you ought to be here?'

'No, sir. I ought to be in with my brother.'

'Oh, you're the twin, are you?' Mr Carton mopped his nose again, looking at Tom without enthusiasm. 'No, for my sins you've been put in with this class. I'm afraid we'll both have to put up with it.'

'What about lunch, sir? Can I meet up with my brother for lunch?'

'Thinking of your stomach already?' Mr Carton was not annoyed, merely amused. 'In this school we stagger the lunch hour so that no more than three classes can flood out the canteen at any one time. You will go for lunch in period eight. If your brother is in class four or six, he may well be in the canteen at that time. If not, no.'

'He's in class three. Does that mean we're never going to meet up?'

'If you're in the same ability range, no doubt you'll be together for Maths, English and French.'

Tom sank back into his seat. It was an odd thing, but though the twins looked identical, with tow-coloured straight hair and blue eyes in round faces, yet Tom was good at English and French, and Davy wasn't. In Maths, it was the other way round.

Tom sniffed.

'Cry baby,' said someone, close by. Tom looked around, prepared to punch someone on the nose, but no one seemed to be paying him any attention.

'Now,' said Mr Carton, 'I want someone to give out these maps of the school, and your timetables. You, boy. You in the front. . . .' He beckoned to a trim lad with a dark skin.

'Stinking Pakis,' someone said. 'This school's full of them.'

It was the Whistler, who could talk out of the side of his mouth.

'What was that?' said Mr Carton.

Everyone looked carefully blank. Tom let his eyes go round the class. There were eight girls in the room, and thirteen boys. Most had dark skins. Later, Tom found out that his class had more than the average number of Sikhs and Pakistanis, with a few West Indians.

There had been coloured children in Tom's previous schools, of course, but he'd never thought anything of it. Now he wondered why. Perhaps it was because the coloured children had been very much in the minority there?

The Whistler caught Tom's eye, and pulled a funny face. Tom smiled back. Tom thought the Whistler was really great, especially when he'd stood up to the teacher like that.

'Now listen, everyone,' said Mr Carton. 'When the bell rings at the end of this lesson, you'll all go as a class to the Maths department to take your first test. Look at your maps and you'll see where the Maths rooms are. Then you come back here for an English test. After that you can stampede through the corridors for lunch in the canteen. Now when I say 'stampede' I don't mean that you're to go charging around knocking down everyone in sight. Save your muscle for the P.E. lesson you'll be having first thing this afternoon. And that reminds me.'

He ran his eyes round the class, sent a glare to the back row where someone was giggling, and then went on.

'We finish dead on three o'clock every afternoon. That is, official lessons finish at that time. But after three o'clock there are various clubs and societies which meet in school for another hour. I want to see all of you sign on for some activity or other. In the corridors you will see a series of notice-boards, one for each club. On these notice-boards are posters saying what each club does and when they meet. If you want to make model train sets, for instance, then you sign up for Thursday nights.

If you want to join the choir, or one of the music groups, then you'll be here almost every afternoon.

'There's sports, of course. We have an excellent sports hall. Our teams have been beating everyone else in the Borough at football, tennis and netball. We'd like some beginners, though. Keep busy, keep out of mischief. That's all I ask.'

The Whistler put his hand up, with a grin. 'Please sir, do we get a black mark, if we don't want to sign up for any of these clubs?'

'No, Gardam. It's not obligatory. You don't have to. But I'm sure you'd enjoy it if you tried. I can't say that you look as if you'd add lustre to our school's football team – though I may be doing you an injustice – but I should think you'd make a useful sprinter. Think about it.'

Tom felt depression settle upon his shoulders. Tom's twin had recently discovered the joys of playing the bassoon, and had been practising to make himself good enough to join the school orchestra. If there were music sessions every afternoon after school, then it looked as if Tom would be on his own then, too.

'One last thing,' said Mr Carton, 'We expect you to work at this school, and we reward hard work with outings to the theatre, end of term parties, and trips abroad. This term, in about a month's time, we're going to take a coach load of you over to France for the day. I'll be getting out a form for you to take home to your parents about this.'

'Please sir,' said the Whistler, in a gravelly, comical voice, 'I can't speak the lingo.'

'You won't need to, Gardam,' said Mr Carton. 'There will be plenty of teachers going with you, and some of you, at least, will have enough French to be able to translate for the others.'

11

'I can speak it a bit,' said Tom to the Whistler, as the bell rang, and they shuffled to their feet.

'Twin!' said the Whistler, making it an insult.

'Yes,' said Tom, feeling sick all over again.

The Whistler punched Tom on the arm. 'You're all right. You stood up to them, anyway.'

Tom felt better at that. 'I did try.'

'That teacher – Box-face – old Carton. He's a charmless nerk. We mustn't let him get us down.'

Tom felt he couldn't have put it better, if he'd tried. Also, he liked that 'we'. It implied that even though he'd been deserted by his twin, other people liked his company.

'School,' said the Whistler, as they crowded out into the corridor with the rest of the class, 'is for the birds. Boring. Puko.'

'To think we're condemned to it for the next four years!'

'Put it there.' The Whistler extended his hand to Tom. They struck each other's hands, and grinned.

Someone spoke up above them. 'Hey, Whistler. Are we staying, or what?'

Tom turned and looked up, and up. The boy towered over them, nearly as tall as the teachers. He was big and strong, with a skin-head short crop of pale hair. He looked at Tom as if he didn't like him, much.

'Oh,' said the Whistler to Tom. 'This is Bongo Harris. He's my bully boy. Aren't you, Bongo? Bongo, this is Tom. He's all right.'

'Hi,' said Tom, meaning to be friendly.

Bongo grunted, and turned back to the Whistler. Bongo was a boy who only had one idea at a time. 'Do we split, then?'

Whistler considered the question. 'No, we case the

joint. See what gives. There may be pickings, you know.'

Tom blinked. He'd never heard anyone talk like this before, outside the telly.

The Whistler grinned at Tom. 'Are you with us?'

'Why not?' said Tom, happy to find a friend so quickly.

2

Tom only caught one glimpse of his twin all that day. When it was time to go home at three o'clock, Tom went to the entrance, hoping to meet Davy there. Instead, his sister Vivien came out and said that Davy would be staying behind to talk to the head of the Music department.

Tom had half-expected this, but he didn't like it. He felt as if half of him had been cut off and the ends were screaming. He kicked a stone halfway across the pavement and wished he were kicking Davy, instead. Had Davy forgotten that he had a brother?

'Oh, come along,' said Vivien to Tom. 'We've got to pick up Sausage from her school on the way home.'

'You pick up Sausage,' said Tom, hating everyone. 'I'm waiting for Davy.'

Vivien shrugged, and went off.

'Who's she?' said the Whistler, who had been leaning against the fence, whistling softly to himself.

'Elder sister.'

'Bossy, elder sisters.'

'You said it.'

Tom leaned against the fence at the Whistler's side, grateful that someone wanted to talk to him.

'I got a sister,' said the Whistler. 'But she's been married and divorced already. My mum looks after her kid, while my sister works. I hate small kids, don't you?'

'Yes,' said Tom, although he really rather liked Sausage, who was still in the Middle School, and he didn't actively dislike Dumpling, the toddler, because Dumpling was a cuddly little thing and always smiled when she saw him.

'Where's your friend Bongo?' said Tom, since the Whistler also appeared to be waiting for someone.

'Got lost, I reckon. Thick as two short planks, Bongo.'

'Then why do you bother with him?' For no one could accuse the Whistler of being thick. He was too sharp for his own good, if anything.

The Whistler shrugged. 'We come on from the same Middle School, and he's useful, if you want anything shifted. He does what he's told.'

Tom thought about that. He didn't always understand the Whistler.

The Whistler said, 'Which school did you come from?'

Tom told him, and the Whistler pulled a face. 'Oh, the Snobs' school.'

'It's not,' said Tom, but even so, he felt uncomfortable. School was just school, wasn't it? The fact that they'd been taught to speak properly and to respect their teachers didn't mean it was a Snobs' school.

'You should have seen our school,' said the Whistler, and gave a thumbs down sign.

Tom nodded. He'd heard that some schools were a bit ropy, and maybe the Whistler talked in that sloppy way because that was what his old school had been like.

Bongo appeared, lumbering along like an old-fashioned steam engine. Apparently he'd lost his blazer.

'Going our way?' said the Whistler to Tom.

15

Tom was about to say that he was waiting for Davy, and then he thought he might as well go with the Whistler and Bongo. After all, they wanted his company, and Davy obviously didn't.

'Sure thing,' he said, and fell in beside the Whistler.

'Well, what was Big School like?' asked Tom's mother, dishing out fish fingers, frozen peas and bread and butter.

'Much as usual,' said Vivien, jumping in to answer though the question had not been addressed to her. She flicked her long dark hair back over her shoulders. 'Except that the sets have all been rearranged, and now we're in the groups which will take O levels and CSEs. I'm in O level sets for everything except Biology, but I hate Biology so that doesn't matter. Oh yes, and Mrs Wright in the Music department wants us to go in for a Festival in the spring, just a small group of us, a chamber orchestra group. She wants to know if Davy is going to be good enough to join us, because we haven't got another bassoon player.'

Davy slurped tomato ketchup onto his fish fingers and said, 'She cornered me in the music lesson, pinned me up against the piano, and put me through the Spanish Inquisition. You should have heard her, Tom. She's a right corker. Mum, she says I've got to keep up with my piano lessons if I want to get anywhere in music, so I suppose I'd better.'

Sausage, whose horizons were bounded by the amount of food she could absorb, piled her fish fingers into a castle, and said, 'We've got a new teacher. She wears her trousers and her shirt top all in one. We can't think how she goes to the loo.'

Mrs Forrester refilled Tom's glass with milk with one hand, while with the other she prevented the Dumpling from climbing out of her high chair.

'What about you, Tom?'

'We've been separated,' said Tom, casting a dark look at his twin. Tom kicked the table, hard, and Vivien shouted at him to watch it.

'Separated?' said their mother, needing three hands to cope with Dumpling and with Sausage, who was asking for yet another slice of bread and butter.

'Davy never even argued about it,' said Tom, allowing his hurt to show.

'Sorry,' said Davy. 'I thought it might happen, so it wasn't a great shock when it did. Viv warned me ages ago. I knew you'd be upset.'

'Why didn't you tell me?' said Tom, nearly bursting with grief at this fresh evidence of treachery on his twin's part.

Now it was Davy's turn to kick the table. He said, 'I tried, but it was only an idea on Viv's part. Not solid fact. I thought it might not happen.'

Vivien said, laying down the law, 'It's better for twins to be separated so that they can each become persons in their own right. Tom, you're better at some things than Davy, and Davy is better at others. So let it happen.'

'Much you care!' shouted Tom. He rushed out of the room, overturning his chair.

No one cared! He wished he were dead!

He pounded up to the bedroom he shared with his brother, and started kicking the furniture about. It made him feel better to kick the furniture, until he kicked too hard, and hurt his foot. Then he sat down on Davy's bed and concentrated on not crying. Boys of twelve didn't cry, and he was nearly twelve.

Davy crashed open the door and came in, to sit on the bed beside his twin. He said, 'Sorry, Toad.'

Everyone in the family had a nickname. The twins had

17

been called the Toads for as long as they could remember. They'd even been called the Toads at their first and middle schools. They rather liked being known as the Toads, because it gave them an excuse for behaving badly if they felt like it.

They weren't really naughty boys, but they were full of mischief and high spirits and when someone said 'Oh, you Toads!' they would laugh and say they were sorry and promise not to do it again.

Now, for the first time, Tom objected to the nickname. 'I'm not a Toad. I'm Forrester, T., and you're Forrester, D. You're in one class, and I'm in another, and they're going to make sure we never meet again!'

'Yes,' said Davy. He was thoughtful about it, but not stricken.

'You don't care,' said Tom.

'Yes, I do. I don't like it, but I can see why they've done it, in a way. I talked to my form teacher about it, and he said that if I was that bad at English and French, I'd better start working hard, to catch you up. He said he supposed I usually let you do my English and French homework, because you were better at it than me, and he said that if I let someone else do my homework, I'd never get on. I could see he was right.'

'Does that mean you're not going to help me with my Maths homework any more?'

Davy let out a big sigh. Keeping his body straight, he fell backwards onto his bed, and lifted his legs into the air.

He said, 'I can keep my knees straight while I count thirty. Can you?'

Tom didn't even want to try, he was too deeply sunk in misery.

Davy got himself right side up and looked about him.

He said, 'We've got to clean up this mess, Mum says. She says the builders are coming tomorrow morning to start work on the loft conversion.'

'But they won't need to come in here.'

'No, but Mum says she's got to bring the books in here, off the landing, and put them under our beds so that the workmen can get up the stairs. And the landing carpet's got to come up and be put in here for the time being. She says we'd better take the china plaque off the door, in case it gets broken.'

Davy went out, took the plaque off the door, and brought it back in. He stood there, looking down at it. The plaque said, 'This is the Toads' room.'

Tom said, in a small voice, 'We're not the Toads any more. We're Forrester, T., and Forrester, D. I don't want that plaque to go back on the door, ever.'

'It's tragic,' said Davy, 'But I know what you mean. Let's take it out into the garden and bury it, before we start on our homework.'

3

'Waiting for your twin?' said the Whistler, in the playground. 'I ran into him this morning, coming out of Woodwork. Hi, I said, and he looked right through me. He's the spitting image of you, isn't he? Even his hair, falling over his right eye, just like yours.'

'Yes, we're always getting mistaken for one another,' said Tom. He fell in beside the Whistler. Bongo walked one pace behind them, which was something which Tom had found difficult to take at first. Then he worked it out that Bongo had the mentality of an intelligent mongrel dog, and that if you treated him as one, Bongo liked it. So Tom fell in beside the Whistler, and accepted the offer of a piece of chewing gum.

'Perhaps,' said Tom, 'I should part my hair on the other side. That music teacher caught me as I was flying down the corridor yesterday, and gave me stick about being late to choir practice. And some big lad said he'd picked up my satchel. He didn't believe me when I said he'd got Davy's.'

'Why don't you have a haircut?' suggested the Whistler.

Tom looked at the Whistler's haircut in silent admiration. It was some hair-do, that. The Whistler's hair had been cut pretty short on top and at the back, but at the front it was greased and trained into a peak shadowing his eyes. It stayed that way, sort of sculptured, all day long. Also, what Tom had at first thought were blackheads in the Whistler's ears, were actually small black studs. Great. Really trendy.

'I like your haircut,' said Tom. 'But I don't think my hair would stick up that way.'

'You use this and that,' said the Whistler. 'But it costs, of course. How much bread do you have?'

Tom groaned. 'Dad's away, and he forgot to give us any pocket money before he went. Mum says she's skint. She promised she'd get some money today from the Post Office, but I bet she forgets.'

'Your Dad's away? Mine is, too. How long did your Dad get?'

Now Tom wasn't stupid but he didn't quite understand what the Whistler meant. Tom's father travelled for a national firm of furniture manufacturers, and he was often away for several days at a time. Nevertheless, the Whistler's enquiry made Tom uneasy.

'He'll be back at the week-end, I think. How about yours?'

The Whistler shrugged. 'Depends on his good behaviour.'

Tom was silent. Surely the Whistler couldn't mean that his father was in prison, could he?

Tom changed the subject. 'Do you realise that we've been here nearly a fortnight? It seems for ever.'

'Stinking school,' said the Whistler, without heat. 'Too many stinking Pakis getting all the perks, currying favour with the teachers. Hey, did you hear what I just said? I said "currying favour"!'

21

He whooped with laughter, and Tom laughed too, because it was funny though maybe not quite fair.

'Oh, they're all right, I suppose,' said Tom.

'Too many of them, that's all. And Wogs. My dad says they all ought to be sent back where they came from, and then there'd be plenty of jobs for us who were born white and British.'

'I hadn't really thought about it before.'

'Making out they're better than us, licking the teacher's boots. Yuk.'

'Yuk,' said Tom, agreeing. It was true that in their form the Pakis and the Sikhs were getting the top places and all the praise. Tom was trying to work hard, but too much had been happening to him, too quickly, and these last few days he'd rather slackened off.

'Stinking school,' said the Whistler, as the bell went for the end of play time. 'The sooner I can leave, the better. What good is it going to do me, anyway? I'll never pass any exams. Stands to reason. None of my family passes exams. I only report each morning because of the French trip. That'll be a bit of all right. If only I can lay my hands on a bit of the ready, it will be more than a bit of all right.'

'How come?'

'You can buy things in France. All sorts of things that you can't get here. Or at least, you can't get them here without questions being asked. You dig?'

Tom nodded, though he didn't really understand. He'd forgotten about the day trip. He'd put his name down for it straight away, and then forgotten about it. Well, that was something to look forward to. And perhaps he'd be able to go with Davy, who was also going on the trip. Or perhaps he'd go with the Whistler anyway, because the Whistler was far more clued up.

'Yeah, I'm really looking forward to that,' said Tom.

Tom's mother was doing her barmy. She'd had a bad day, with workmen tramping through the house, banging and crashing, and dust flying everywhere. There wasn't a room in the place which hadn't been invaded by some extra piece of furniture or carpeting or a pile of pictures taken down from the staircase. Dumpling had fallen over a pile of torn-out lengths of wood and hurt her knee, Sausage had raided the fridge and got clean away with the apple pie meant for supper, and Mr Forrester was away again.

'Tom, come down here, this minute!' She stood at the bottom of the stairs and screamed till Tom appeared. Davy was moodily practising his bassoon in the downstairs study, Dumpling was emptying a packet of cornflakes over the living-room carpet, and both the telly and the radio were on, full strength.

'Come on down!' shouted Mrs Forrester. 'You've got to take Vivien to choir practice, wait till she's finished, and bring her back.'

Tom's jaw dropped. 'Why?'

'Because there's a dirty old man going around frightening young girls in the neighbourhood, and your father says Vivien's not to go out after dark by herself.'

'Why can't Davy go?'

'He's got to practise.'

'Well, I've got homework too, haven't I?'

'Now don't argue! Get your mac on, and take your homework with you if you're that keen.'

'I can't see why Viv has to go to choir practice at this time of night,' said Tom, reluctantly getting ready. Vivien was already waiting for him by the door, neatly buttoned into her winter mac. 'Doesn't she get enough of that in the daytime at school?'

'It's not at school, stupid,' said Vivien. 'It's at church.

My friend is in the church choir and she says I can join, if I can pass an audition. They sing really good stuff, and I'm to have a choir gown and maybe a medal on a coloured ribbon if I'm good enough.'

'Church?' said Tom, shattered. 'You don't really want to go to church, do you? Of all the boring . .'

'It's not boring,' said Vivien, quickly. 'Or at least, I don't think so. My friend says this church isn't boring at all, that they've got lots of young people, and youth groups and outings, and the vicar's got children of our age. So there.'

Tom followed Vivien down the path and out into the darkening street. 'You don't mean you're taking it seriously?'

'Why not? I'm a Christian, aren't I?'

'But it mucks up Sundays, that's why. Reading the Bible in private is one thing, and I'll say that much for you, you don't preach at us. But you don't have to ruin the family's one day together, do you?'

Vivien didn't answer for some time. Tom trudged along beside her, hoping she'd decide she'd made a mistake so that they could go back and watch the quiz on the telly.

'What I think is,' said Vivien, 'that you can get so far by yourself, and after that you need to be with other people who are also learning about God.'

'But what's the point of it all? It's stupid, if you ask me.'

'It helps me, Tom. That's why.'

She wasn't being bossy, for once. She was speaking to him as if they were the same age, and that wasn't usual with her, either. She was normally a right little bossy boots.

They slowed down as they reached the corner by the

church, and looked at it in silence. Tom remembered how he'd felt, the first time he'd had to walk into a strange class by himself. Luckily he'd had the Whistler with him, for the Whistler was bright enough. Tom and the Whistler were the only white boys who'd made it into the second from the top set in English from their class. It had made an extra bond between them. Now Tom could see that Vivien wasn't happy about walking into this strange church by herself.

He felt sorry for her, almost.

She said, 'My friend said she'd meet me here, outside.'

They looked up and down the street. There was no one there they knew. Various young people and grownups, too, were going into the church, or into the hall at the side of the church. They all seemed to know one another. Tom and Vivien waited and waited, but still Vivien's friend didn't come.

'I'll come in with you, if you like,' said Tom. 'It'll be warmer inside, anyway.'

Vivien didn't thank him, but ploughed straight in with Tom at her heels. Just as Tom had thought, a whole roomful of people turned their heads to look at them. Vivien said coolly enough that her friend had wanted her to audition for the choir. A hard-faced woman got up and pushed everyone along till she'd found Vivien and Tom a seat.

'Sing along with us this evening, and see how you fit in,' she said, handing Vivien and Tom some sheets of music.

'Not for me,' said Tom, scurrying away to the back of the vestry in which the practice was being held.

'Don't you sing, then?' said the choirmistress.

'You must be joking!' said Tom, who sang pretty well, but was against this church lark on principle. He found himself a corner and sat down to do his homework.

Luckily it wasn't difficult homework tonight. He zipped through that, and then looked for his reading book, only to discover that he'd left it behind. He looked around for something else to read. The choir was doing something that wailed up and down. Awful row, Tom thought.

He'd go mad if he didn't find something to read. He picked up a book and opened it at random. It was a psalm book; not that Tom knew what psalms were, then.

Tom got interested. Lovely blood and thunder. Curses to your enemies! Grind their bones and so on and so forth. That was a bit of all right, Tom thought.

He turned a couple of pages, and some words leapt out of the page at him.

'. . . a gang of evil men is round me; like a pack of dogs they close in on me . . .'

Wow, thought Tom. That was just like the hero in that Western film he'd been watching on the telly the other night when his dad had thought he was in bed.

That was hot stuff. He rolled the phrase around his tongue, but got bothered by the silly stuff the choir was singing at the same time. His concentration went.

He got bored, and tipped his chair back to look up at the ceiling. He wondered how much longer he was going to have to put up with all this. He realised, with considerable annoyance, that if Viv was going to join this choir, someone was going to have to bring her every week, and sit through all this wailing stuff.

Cats' noises weren't in it.

He looked at his watch and sighed, shaking his whole body, and nearly falling off the chair. The choir started on something different.

'The Lord is my shepherd, I shall not want . . .'

Now that's more like, thought Tom. That had a good

tune to it, the sort of tune you could remember. Perhaps he could teach it to the Whistler, who couldn't read a note of music, but could whistle anything, once he'd heard it.

Tom wondered if he could get the Whistler to share guard-dog duty on Viv with him, and then told himself not to be stupid, because the Whistler wouldn't want to get mixed up in anything so boring. The Whistler spent most of his evenings down at the amusement arcade in the High Street. Sometimes the attendant would let the Whistler give out change, and once, with Bongo as bouncer, the attendant had gone out and left the whole amusement arcade in the Whistler's charge for an hour. Now that was something!

Tom wished he were with the Whistler, and not sitting there, listening to other people going on about God. For crying out loud! No one but dumbos believed in God nowadays. All that sort of thing went out with the Ark!

At the end of choir practice, Vivien was given a voice test, and told to report on Sunday morning, a quarter of an hour before the service. The choirmistress asked Tom to sing a couple of bars of a hymn for her, but Tom, who had no intention of being roped into the choir, deliberately sang off-key.

When they got out, Vivien said, 'I suppose you thought that was clever! Especially after I told her that you had a nice voice.'

'You didn't think I was going to get tied up with that lot, did you?'

'At least it would get you away from the Whistler.'

'What's wrong with the Whistler?'

'What's right with him?'

'He's got more life in him than any of your stuffed-up dummies who talk with plums in their mouths and can't say boo to a goose. And how about that 'friend' of yours who was supposed to meet you here tonight? She let you down, didn't she? Well, the Whistler wouldn't let me down, if he'd promised to meet me.'

'If you'd been listening, you'd have heard that she rang the choirmistress to say she couldn't come because she's got a tummy bug.'

'I did listen. Miaow, miaow! That's all I heard.'

Vivien aimed a blow at him with her new choir folder. He ducked and moved out of range.

'Miaow, miaow!'

'Toad!'

'I'm not a Toad now. I'm Forrester, T., and you'd better mind your manners, or I'll set Bongo on to you.'

'I just bet you would!'

'Well, the Whistler would, anyway. He said to me, "Tom, if you need some muscle any time, you tell me, and I'll get Bongo onto it." I've got friends now, see. I don't need you, and I don't need Davy any more.'

'Some friends! Everyone knows the Whistler's a jail-bird.'

'He is not!'

'Well, his father is, anyway. Someone in the orchestra told me. He's been sent away, they said, for burglary.'

Tom wanted to deny it, but something stuck in his throat. Was it true? Could it be true? He felt bereaved, all over again. First Davy had deserted him, and now his clever friend the Whistler turned out to have a criminal for a father. Tom felt cold. He shivered.

'Didn't you know?' said Vivien, nose in the air.

'No, I didn't,' said Tom. 'But it doesn't make any difference.'

It did, of course, But when Tom thought of life at school without the Whistler's cheerful nonsense, he knew that he could be a lot worse off than he was.

28

'He's all right,' said Tom, quietly. 'The Whistler's a good friend to me, and it's not his fault if his father's in prison. Lay off him, Viv.'

'I'll lay off him, if you lay off me. I'd rather have God for a friend than your Whistler, any day.'

'Miaow, miaow!' said Tom.

4

There are days when everything goes wrong, and this was one of them. Tom had lost his dinner money, and torn the lining of his blazer so that he couldn't get it on or off without a struggle. Now the Whistler dropped his English homework in the corridor, and he had to watch it being ground to pulp by a herd of schoolchildren changing classes.

In the scuffle to retrieve the book, Tom had his elbow banged. He turned his face to the wall, so that no one could see tears in his eyes.

'That's done it,' said the Whistler. 'I've had it, up to here!'

Tom smoothed out the ragged remains of the Whistler's homework. 'Look, I'll explain to the teacher . . .'

'He won't believe you. You know how he picks on me.'

Now this was true enough to make Tom hesitate.

'Me mum can't say I didn't try,' said the Whistler, in a choked up sort of voice. 'Three weeks I've tried. I've turned up on time, I've done me homework, and I've kept me nose clean. And what happens? I'm picked on.'

'What else can we do?' said Tom.

'Bunk off, of course.' The Whistler looked up and down the now empty corridor, and slid sideways out of a door into the playground. With a sense of adventure Tom followed. The Whistler hissed at Tom to keep in the lee of the wall. They edged under the window of a classroom, turned a corner and darted across an empty playground area into the shadow of the Science block.

'Where are we going?' whispered Tom.

'Hush!' The Whistler gave quick glances around. 'Behind the Sports Hall. That's where the Club meets.'

'What Club?'

'To smoke, of course.'

Tom's eyes opened wide, and he followed the Whistler with renewed zest. Tom's dad had said he'd tan their hides if he caught any of his children smoking, and what with his threat and being short of pocket money, neither Tom nor Davy had got into that particular activity as yet. Which wasn't to say that they weren't curious about it. They were, intensely curious.

Between the Sports Hall and the wire fence that bounded the school grounds there were some scrubby bushes and half-grown trees. The ground was beaten bare underfoot, and although a lot of leaves had fallen from the branches by now, there was still enough cover for two boys to make themselves inconspicuous. Empty fag packets and coke tins littered the place, showing that it was much used, but at that moment Tom and the Whistler had it to themselves.

The Whistler dragged a packet from the inside pocket of his blazer, together with a book of matches, and handing a cigarette to Tom, they lit up.

The Whistler smoked as if he were used to it, pushing out his lower jaw, and holding the cigarette between his teeth. With his eyes narrowed, he was, perhaps, imitating Humphrey Bogart.

Tom put the cigarette to his lips and took a quick puff. Then he held it in his hand, admiring the way the smoke curled up into the autumn sky.

'No,' said the Whistler, continuing some argument he'd been having with himself. 'Me mum can't blame me. Really she can't. Everyone's against me.'

Tom let the words rise to his tongue, without really thinking what he was saying. '"Like a gang of evil men around me, like a pack of dogs they close in on me."'

The Whistler looked startled. 'That's some poetry!'

'It's from a book I was reading the other night.' Tom wasn't brave enough to say that he'd read it in church.

'What book?'

'A book of songs. It's all right. Lots of curses.'

'I could do with some new curses. I've run out of old ones.'

'These are old ones, but they don't use bad language.' Tom threw his head back, trying to remember some more. '"They open their mouths like lions, roaring and tearing at me. My strength is gone, like water spilt on the ground . . . Oh Lord, come quickly to my rescue. . . ."'

'What was that?' The Whistler was sharp.

'" Come quickly to my rescue,"' said Tom, confused. 'It's just a poem, or something. A psalm, I think they call it.'

The Whistler grunted, and there was silence while Tom's blush faded. The Whistler hadn't seen him blush, luckily. The Whistler was puffing away at his cigarette like he was making Indian smoke signals.

'Me mum used to be religious,' said the Whistler, unexpectedly. 'She stopped, when she married me dad. She didn't even bother to have me done.'

'Done?'

'Christened. She had me elder sister done, but when it come to me, she couldn't be bothered. Me dad was dead against it, see. Me mum had had enough hassle, getting me sister done. She didn't bother with me. Have you been done?'

'Christened? Yes. My sister Viv goes to church now. She's joined the church choir, and Mum makes me take her and bring her back. They wanted me to join the church choir as well, but I sang flat.'

'Me mum used to pray, at nights. When Dad had hit her, and all.'

Tom was silent, respecting the Whistler's confidence. He was sorry for the Whistler and also, he really liked him. There was something about a boy who could get kicked around like the Whistler was, and still bob up ready to try and try again. And be cheerful about it.

The Whistler pulled out some sandwiches and a can of Coke. He shared them with Tom. Yesterday Tom had had an apple and had shared it with the Whistler. In the old days, Tom would have shared with Davy. It wasn't the same, with the Whistler, but it was good. Perhaps in some ways it was even better, because the Whistler didn't have to go around with Tom but had chosen to do so.

Tom said, 'They've got a youth club, down at the church. Every time I go to choir with Viv, she's on at me, to join the youth club.'

It was an invitation to the Whistler in a way. The Whistler considered it, found it too much to cope with, and gracefully declined.

'I gotta help out at the Amusement Arcade, see. And Bongo, he'll get into trouble if I'm not there to keep an eye on him.'

'What sort of trouble?'

'He's thick, and he likes to fight. Fighting gets him the last word, see. But if I'm there, I can usually talk him out of it.'

That was another good thing about the Whistler; he looked after Bongo as if he were his younger brother.

The Whistler said, 'You won't tell anyone, will you?'

'No. What?'

'Me dad's lost his remission.'

Tom didn't say anything to that. He had found it hard to accept the Whistler's background, so different from his own. In one way, Tom was ashamed of his friend. And in another way, Tom felt that knowing the Whistler was helping him to grow up, to learn things he would never have learned otherwise.

Tom said, 'I won't tell anyone.'

'I can't talk about it to anyone else.'

'Didn't you have any friends, before you came here?'

'In the old school? Yes, I knocked around with the usual crowd. Of course I did. Everyone did. It wasn't like your old school. It was rough. Some of me old mates came on to this school, but they're not in our class and they're not in our sets, either. I see them about, up at the Arcade, and in the Square, at nights. But me mum said when I come here, she said I could make a fresh start where no one knew. She made me promise to try.'

'You have tried.'

'The teachers know,' said the Whistler, frowning. 'And they pick on me. You've seen them. And sometimes I could just kick the lot in. Skive off.'

'But you don't. Why, you're really clever, Whistler. You're brighter than I am at English and Maths, and you're catching up in French. You could do anything, get your O levels, maybe even go to University.'

34

'What, me?' The Whistler gave a hard laugh. 'With my dad? And my mum? You ain't seen them, Tom.'

'Try me.'

The Whistler said, looking hard at the sky. 'Me mum says you could come round one evening now, before me dad gets back. But you won't like it. Our place is a dump.'

'You said you'd got a video, and a big colour TV and a music centre.'

'For the moment. It's all on the never-never, and who knows how long we'll keep it? And me mum's too tired to cook for us, what with her jobs and looking after the kid.'

'I'll come, anyway. I'd like to. And I'll ask my mum when you can come round to our place.'

'Will she mind?'

Tom went red. 'I just remembered that it'll have to be after the builders have finished with the loft conversion. The mess, you wouldn't believe!'

'Oh, of course,' said the Whistler, meaning that he didn't really expect to be invited, after all.

'Cheer up,' said Tom. 'Things can only get better.'

'"From things that go bump in the night,"' said the Whistler, suddenly, '"Good Lord, deliver us". Me mum used to say that to me, when I was a kid. Do you think that's from your psalm book?'

'Dunno. Tell you what. I'll borrow one of their books when I next take Viv to choir, and we'll have a look through.'

'What was that bit about the roaring lions?'

Tom said, his mind racing ahead, '"Oh Lord, come quickly to my rescue..."'

'That's all right,' said the Whistler in a dissatisfied voice, 'if you believe. It's no good saying it, if you don't believe, is it?'

'I don't know,' said Tom, equally disturbed. 'Perhaps it might be, if you sort of half-believed. Or believed a bit of the time.'

The Whistler was looking to Tom for help, and Tom searched the back of his mind for something helpful to say. The words came into his mind, and he let them come out.

'"Yea, though I walk through the valley of the shadow of death, I shall fear no evil." It's from a hymn they were singing the other night. I looked it up, and it's different in the modern version but almost as nice. "Even if I go through the deepest darkness I will not be afraid, Lord, for you are with me."'

The Whistler looked all around him, as if expecting someone to materialise like a ghost. 'That sent a prickle all down my back.'

'It doesn't "prickle" me,' said Tom. 'But it does make me think. I've been thinking about it a lot, as a matter of fact. You won't let on to the others about it, will you? They'd only laugh.'

'I'm not laughing,' said the Whistler. 'It's not a laughing matter, is it?'

5

'Hold hard!' The voice came from somewhere above Tom's head. He looked up and up, and found a tall man was bending over him, looking at Tom as if he were an interesting experiment in science. That beaky nose and plasticine-like face were a well-known sight in the school. Tom gulped. No one, but no one, played around with the Deputy Head, Mr Bird.

'Dicky' Bird was reputed to have a computer in his brain. Once he'd heard something about you, he never forgot. He was always quietly spoken, never bothered about the bells which governed the rest of the school, and it was said he could reduce even the toughest bully boy to tears inside three minutes.

So Tom gulped.

'Now which of the twins are you?' asked the Bird.

'Please sir, Forrester T.'

'First name?'

'Tom.'

'Ah yes. Davy Forrester has pointed ears, now I come to think of it. Well, Tom, I've been meaning to have a chat with you. Come along to my office.'

The bell had gone for the end of the day, and Tom had

been careering along the corridor along with everyone else, when the Bird had caught him. Tom looked around for the Whistler, and saw him slide through the nearest door into a vacant classroom. Maybe the Whistler would wait for him, maybe not.

'This way,' said the Bird, guiding Tom into a pleasant room by the main entrance. He indicated that Tom should sit in a comfortable chair, and took a seat himself. 'How are you finding things, now you've had a chance to settle down?'

'All right, sir.' What else did the Bird expect him to say?

'I hear you were upset at being separated from your twin. Mr Carton was worried that you might not find it easy to settle down in such a big school, without leaning on your brother all the time. So I told him I'd have you in for a chat after a few weeks, to see how you were coping.'

'I'm all right, sir.'

'I had a word with your brother the other day, in choir practice. He seems to have found his level, all right. A hard worker, they tell me. Good at Maths, and average in everything else. Quite different from you, apart from looks. Is that right?'

'Yes, sir.' So rumour had spoken the truth, and the Bird did know everything. Tom looked at the door for help, because he had an uneasy feeling he knew where this conversation was leading.

'Are you in a hurry?'

'No, sir.' Tom took his eyes off the door, and looked at the wall behind the Bird. A cross hung there. Tom's gaze sharpened. Was the Bird a Christian, too? Did he go to church? Did he know that verse about the pack of dogs closing in around him?

'I hear,' said the Bird, pushing one side of his face up

till his eyes went squinty, 'that you've found yourself a new friend to take Davy's place in your life.'

Tom felt his breath catch in his throat. Everyone was against his being friends with the Whistler. Mr Carton was openly disapproving, so was Viv; and even his mum had had a go at him, wanting him to make a more 'suitable' friend. Tom's chin came out. He didn't say anything, but he looked a lot.

The Bird said, 'Now I'm not one to jump to conclusions. Suppose you tell me about it.'

Tom wondered if he could get away with playing the innocent. He looked at the Bird's wise eyes, and decided he couldn't. He was silent.

The Bird coughed. 'Do your parents like this new friend of yours?'

Tom winced. Of course they didn't. And the Bird must know it.

'Well, sir; he's been brought up a little differently from me, but he learns fast. I don't think that really matters.'

'What does matter?' You couldn't shake the Bird off. He really wanted to know.

Tom took a deep breath. Perhaps even as long ago as yesterday, he'd not have been able to stand up to this, but now he could. Courage had come from somewhere. Maybe it had come from remembering that psalm about being surrounded by dogs tearing at you.

Tom looked the Bird straight in the eye, and said, 'You think he's a bad influence on me. You think he's going to lead me into bad ways. That's what Mr Carton and the other teachers think. They try to sit us on opposite sides of the class and they look disapproving if they see us in the playground together. That's silly.'

'You mean, that if they stopped disapproving, you'd

not be so insistent about being with the Whistler all the time?'

Tom frowned. 'No, I don't mean that. I mean that I really like the Whistler. He thinks for himself.'

'Ah,' said the Bird, and leaned back in his chair. 'Now I agree with you, there. It's very rare, isn't it, to find a boy of your age who can think for himself. Do you approve of all his ideas?'

Tom blinked. Now he came to think about it, Tom didn't approve of all the Whistler's ideas. Tom said, cautiously, 'Sometimes we argue, but we don't quarrel. He listens, when I want to say something, and the other way round. We're both learning, all the time. It's harder for him to get on, than it is for me. It's harder for him to do his homework, because he's got nowhere quiet to sit in the evenings. . . .'

'I wasn't talking about homework. Or perhaps I was.'

Tom's heart began to go at it, really fast. He said, 'Suppose it's not him who's a bad influence on me, but the other way round! Suppose I'm good for him?'

Tom thought he'd gone too far, for the silence went on and on. Tom felt a nervous gulp start in his throat. It turned into a choke. He coughed and felt himself going red. He looked at the cross, and thought about his enemies opening their mouths like lions, and the Lord coming quickly to the rescue.

The Bird said, 'You have to be very strong to help other people, Tom. You have to give yourself over and over again, and at the same time you have to stand fast on what you think is right. Even when people laugh at you. Even if they threaten you.'

In that moment Tom took a big leap forward in understanding people. He looked at the Bird, and saw that the Bird had been describing himself.

The Bird put his fingertips together, and looked at Tom over them. 'Have you ever said "no" to anything the Whistler has suggested you should do?'

'I don't think so, sir.'

'Has he ever suggested your doing something which you've been uneasy about?'

'No, sir.' Tom lied, and he knew it. That cigarette, and bunking off, and maybe one or two other little incidents. Tom told himself not to blush and knew that he was.

'Well one day, sooner or later, the Whistler may suggest that you do something a bit shady. He may not see any harm in it, because that's the way he's always done things. I'm not saying he's a bad boy, but that he's not always been taught the difference between good and bad. Do you follow me?'

'Yes, sir.' Grimly.

'The question is, Tom; can you say "no" when the time comes?'

Silence. Tom wasn't sure.

The Bird said, 'Much older men and women have fallen down on this problem, Tom. It's a tough one. Maybe you're not ready to tackle it yet. Perhaps I ought to move you into another form. . . .'

'No, sir.' That would be quite wrong, Tom knew that. He looked at the cross for inspiration, and the Bird saw where he was looking.

The Bird said, 'Are you a Christian?'

Tom hesitated. 'I don't think so, sir. We're sort of looking at the question together, the Whistler and I. I don't think I'm a Christian yet, sir. I just can't quite bring myself to believe in it.'

'Doubting Thomas,' said the Bird. 'Look it up. John chapter 20. Well, now. If you've got that far, Tom, I think we'll leave this in the Lord's hands. But I want you to do some hard thinking about it. Promise me?'

The Bird stood up, and held out his hand. Tom shook hands with the Bird, and walked out into the corridor, feeling as if he'd just stepped on a landmine, and been hurled into the air.

The Whistler was waiting for him, outside. 'What did he want?'

Tom shook his head, to clear it. 'That was head-banging stuff, Whistler. He's. . . . gosh.'

'Are you running out on me, then?'

'No, but I need to be quiet, to think.'

The Whistler pushed his face close to Tom. 'Because, if you're thinking of running out on me, I'd do something about it.'

'Such as?' Tom wasn't frightened. He was too preoccupied for that.

'I'd get some of my old pals and Bongo, and I'd show you. That's what.'

'Oh, don't be daft!' Tom couldn't believe in threats like that.

The Whistler grinned. 'I tell you straight, I'd do it, if you ran out on me.'

'But I won't.'

'Coming, then?' The Whistler tipped his head towards the main road.

'No, I'm late and Mum'll give me stick. Also I've got to look something up in a book. Why don't you come home with me, instead? It's chaos, with the builders still in, but I don't think Mum will mind, and Davy's not going to be back for a while, because he's got orchestra.'

Tom had a feeling his mother might not be very pleased to have the Whistler walk in on them, but the offer had been made, and Tom wouldn't go back on it.

The Whistler took out a comb and passed it through his hair. Tom wished, oh, how he wished, that his own hair would behave like the Whistler's. Tom needed a haircut. His tow-coloured mop had gone all shaggy and was over his ears. Perhaps he could persuade his mother to send him to the Whistler's hairdresser. And pigs might fly.

'Does she make cakes for tea?' asked the Whistler.

6

Viv didn't bring her friends home for tea, and neither did Sausage. Tom had never brought anyone home before because he'd not needed anyone but Davy.

The family were wary of the Whistler. Tom could see them suspending judgement and making allowances like mad. They were all very polite to the Whistler. Perhaps too polite. When Viv and Davy got back, they stared at the Whistler and said they'd got a lot of homework to do in the study after tea.

So Tom took the Whistler up to the bedroom he shared with Davy, and they settled down to their own homework together.

This, thought Tom, was great. Davy was inclined to mess about, and grumble for ages before he got down to work, but the Whistler was like Tom; eyes down and get it over and done with.

The room was a bit of a mess, with piles of books everywhere, and a roll of carpet in front of the cupboard. The Whistler sat by the window, and Tom sat at his desk, and they worked on a short poem, for their English teacher.

The poem had to be really short, not more than a hundred words, and it had to be about themselves.

The Whistler finished first. 'How about this?

> "If I were a kite
> I'd break my string
> and fly away.
> Maybe I'd get burned
> up in the sun,
> but that would be
> better than being
> tied down to earth
> all the time."'

'Gosh!' said Tom. 'That's really good.'

The Whistler looked pleased. He said, 'In the old school, I'd never have dared to write about things I felt. It would have been puko. What have you written?'

Tom frowned. He was having trouble with his poem.

'It's gone into three lines, and I can't add anything to make it longer. It says, 'I wish I could believe. Maybe I could. Doubting Thomas.'

The Whistler said, 'Does that mean what I think it means?'

Tom picked up Vivien's Bible, which he'd borrowed on his way up the stairs, and read out the story of Doubting Thomas, who wouldn't believe Christ had risen, until he had put his hands on our Lord's wounds.

The Whistler listened with a shiny look in his eyes. Then his eyes went hard and blank and he said, 'That's too hard for me.'

Tom gave him an old-fashioned look. 'You know what that means as well as I do. You're not dumb.'

'Well, it's not for the likes of you and me, is it?'

'Why not?' said Tom.

The Whistler aimed a blow at Tom's head. 'Get your hair cut, you hairy monster!'

They went into a scrimmage, which finished that conversation.

Later Tom wandered up the new, sweet-smelling wood staircase and opened the unpainted doors at the top. The workmen had finished the main structure of the loft conversion, and were now working on the outside. Soon the plasterers would come, and after that, they could put a coat of paint over everything, and then move the furniture up.

To Tom's right was a new bathroom, with holes where the fitments would eventually go. To his left was a room overlooking the street, which Sausage was going to occupy. Straight ahead was the door into what would one day be Vivien's room. She hadn't waited for the plasterers and the painters, but had moved a stool and her music stand up there already. She was sitting in the room now with her oboe, playing over some scales in the bright bare space.

'What do you want?' she said, not unkindly, but busy with her practising.

'Dunno,' said Tom, hunching his shoulders up to his ears.

'Has that friend of yours gone? Really, Tom! Couldn't you latch on to someone decent for a change?'

'What's wrong with the Whistler?' Yet Tom knew very well what was wrong with him.

'The Bible says you should avoid bad company.'

'He's very good company,' said Tom, wilfully misunderstanding her.

'You have to take a long spoon if you sup with the Devil.'

Tom got angry. 'Isn't there anything in that Bible of yours about being nice to people who are finding it hard to be good?'

46

Viv looked at him, really looked at him. Usually she gave him a sort of glazed-over, don't-bother-me-now sort of look.

She said, 'You're not really like Davy, are you? I mean, you look like him but you don't sound like him, and you think quite different thoughts.'

'I'm me,' said Tom, still annoyed. 'And I want help with the Whistler.' He hadn't known he was going to ask for help, and he was amazed at himself for approaching Viv about it. She was, after all, the most priggish, sarcastic girl he knew.

She went all wide-eyed on him. She even put down her oboe, to think over what he'd said.

Tom went on, 'The Bird called me in today. He wanted to know what I'd do if the Whistler asked me to do something I ought not to do. The Bird understands why I want to go on being friends with the Whistler, and I thought you might, too.'

He'd thought nothing of the sort, but maybe now she'd stopped being the bossy elder sister, she might understand.

Viv said, sounding different, 'There are bits in the Bible about sinners repenting, and black sheep returning to the fold. All sorts of stories about them. Why don't you look them up? And you could pray for him, too.'

Tom felt as if she'd kicked him. 'What, me? Pray? Don't be daft!'

'Why not? It works. And remember the sparrows. "Not one sparrow is forgotten by God." That means you and me.'

'Sparrows? That's girls' talk. You can't expect me to think of myself as a sparrow.'

'Have it your own way,' said Viv, lifting her oboe to her mouth again. 'Now if you don't mind, I'm busy.'

'Mum, I need a haircut, and I haven't had my pocket money for ever.'

'I'm a bit short, but my purse is on the table,' said Mrs Forrester, mopping up after Dumpling, who had managed to tip the washing-up water all over the kitchen floor.

'How much can I take?' asked Tom, rummaging in the purse. There was a fiver, and some coins, amounting to nearly another pound.

'I owe Viv and Davy theirs as well, but I don't think I've got enough change. Take the fiver, get your haircut in the Lane, and then you can give Viv and Davy their money out of the change.'

'They're at the Saturday morning music school.'

'That's all right. You can give it to them at lunch-time.'

What Tom really wanted was to get a haircut which would make him look different from Davy, but Tom wasn't sure he could get that in the Lane, because the barber in the Lane was so old he hadn't even heard of a blow-dry yet.

If you asked that old man for anything modern, he'd say 'What?' and give you the same old back-and-sides. The only good thing about him was that he only charged a pound for a haircut.

Would his mum mind if he spent more than a pound for once? Tom was meeting the Whistler in the High Street in ten minutes. Perhaps the Whistler would go with him to the barber's, and help him get a new haircut. Tom transferred all the money from his mother's purse into his pocket and walked quickly out of the house so that he shouldn't think about what he was doing.

'I dare you!' said the Whistler, laughing.

'Oh, I couldn't!' said Tom, also laughing.

'It'll grow out quickly enough,' said the Whistler.

'Now's your chance to get away from that stuffy snob's image.'

Tom hesitated, and was lost. The Whistler took him into the fashionable hairdressers, and did the talking.

Half an hour later Tom walked out, penniless, feeling very bare and cold about the ears and the sides of his head. His taffy-coloured hair had been partly shaved off, and the remainder stiffened into a cockscomb over the top of his head. He looked at himself in shop windows as they walked along. He felt unreal, floaty.

He couldn't stop grinning. He didn't look like Davy any more. He looked like the Whistler's friend.

He thought of Viv's and Davy's pocket money which he'd spent, and for a moment or two, he panicked. Then he grinned again. This would show them!

He went back with the Whistler to his council flat. The Whistler borrowed his mum's darning needle and pierced Tom's ears. Tom tried not to wriggle, or to screw up his eyes, because it did hurt, a bit. But when the Whistler lent Tom a pair of his cast-off studs, Tom felt he didn't mind.

'I'm a real masher,' he said. 'Dinko!'

'Urgh!' said the Whistler, pretending to be sick. Then they both fell about, laughing.

'Will you look at him!' shouted Davy. He dragged Tom into the living-room, and thrust him forward.

Tom tried to keep a cocky smile on his face, but found it difficult. It was one thing to peacock about the streets with the Whistler, and another to show off his Mohican and pierced ears before his family.

His father was home, deep in an armchair, reading the newspaper. Sausage was laying out a train set on the floor at his feet, and the Dumpling was fast asleep on the settee.

49

'Oh, dear!' said Tom's mum, wiping her hands on her apron. She looked as if she were going to cry.

Tom's father shouted with laughter. 'Well, I never; wotcha, cock!'

'It's a bit of all right, isn't it?' said Tom, trying to brazen it out.

Davy walked around him, making whooping Indian war cries.

'Shut it!' said Tom, showing Davy a clenched fist.

'Oh, dear, oh dear!' said Tom's mum, sitting down heavily.

Sausage said, 'Well, I think it looks silly!'

Tom said to his father, 'I didn't want to look like Davy any more.'

'That's all very well,' said his father, sobering up, 'But haven't you gone a little far? What will they say at school? Do they allow you to go around like that?'

'It'll grow out quickly enough,' said Tom, affecting carelessness. Actually he was no longer sure it had been a good idea to have a Mohican, but he would have died rather than admit it.

'I've been waiting for you to get back,' said Viv, bouncing into the room. 'Where's my pocket money? Mum says you took a fiver, to get change.'

'I. . . .' Tom shut his mouth on excuses, and stood silent.

'Oh dear!' said his mother. 'I knew no good would come of having the Whistler around! Oh, Tom; you've never spent their money as well, have you?'

'Not exactly,' said Tom, uneasily. 'I just borrowed it. I'm sorry about that but I'll repay it, honest.'

'You're a thief!' shouted Davy. 'I don't want you as a brother, either! I wish you weren't my brother! I wish you were dead!'

'Calm down, all of you,' said Mr Forrester. 'I think it's funny, but Tom, you have gone too far, you know. If you'd explained to your mother . . .'

'Would she have let me do it?'

'No, of course I wouldn't', said Mrs Forrester, fishing for her handkerchief.

'I'd have understood,' said Tom's father, and it really looked as if he might have done so. 'But you've been and gone and done it, the wrong way. You'd better apologise for a start, Tom.'

'I'm sorry!' shouted Tom. 'I hate all of you!' And he rushed upstairs to his room to kick the furniture about.

7

Davy came into the twins' bedroom, and scowled at Tom.

Davy said, 'I want to work in here. If you're going to stay, you'll have to be quiet!'

'Miaow, miaow!' said Tom. He rushed out of the room, and pounded up the stairs to the unfinished top floor. Several boxes of books and some rolls of carpet had already been thrown into the main bedroom, and Vivien's music stand and stool had come to a permanent resting place by the window.

The windows were closed, double-glazed, curtainless. Tom caught sight of himself in the window, against the darkness of the wintry afternoon outside, and he winced. He'd not recognised himself for a moment. Perhaps – awful thought – perhaps the family were right, and he'd been really stupid to get a Mohican. Also, it felt cold about his ears. And his ears hurt, where they'd been pierced.

Tom's father came softly but heavily up the stairs, and walked into the room.

'Well,' said Tom, kicking the nearest roll of carpet, 'I said I was sorry.'

Tom's father sat on the stool. 'Now, suppose you tell me all about it.'

So Tom started. He began with the first day at the school, and he went on and on, pouring it all out, about how awful the Whistler's home life was, and about how the teachers were all down on him, and Bongo being so helpless and stupid, and even about the forbidden cigarette, and lastly the talk with the Bird.

Then Tom stopped and looked at his father. His father wasn't looking cross, but he was looking worried.

Tom said, defiantly, 'I've never had a friend of my own before. You can't count Davy because he didn't choose me, and I didn't choose him. I never thought I'd have to look for another friend but now it's happened, and we're getting so different in the way we look at things, it seems that Davy and I will never be friends again. But the Whistler is something else. Even the Bird saw what I meant about the Whistler, and he hasn't separated us or anything.'

Mr Forrester sighed. He didn't seem to know what to say.

Tom went on, 'I know what you're thinking. You think I can't say "no" to the Whistler, and that one day he might lead me into real trouble. Not just skiving off for the odd cigarette . . .'

'I've been half expecting that to crop up. It's not a good idea for you to start smoking, especially when you can't afford it, but it's not a major crime.'

'Nor is having a haircut!'

Mr Forrester grinned. 'That was just stupid. Isn't it rather cold?'

'No,' said Tom. But it was, of course.

'It'll lead to trouble at school. They may suspend

53

you, till you look normal. But that's not what really worries me. You stole the money for it.'

Tom winced. It hadn't been stealing, exactly. He was silent, eyes on his scuffed shoes.

'Well, Tom?' said his father. 'We can't just let that slide, can we?'

Tom shook his head. No, in justice, they couldn't let that slide.   Mr Forrester sighed. 'It's not just the loss of the money, though as you know, we're feeling the pinch, what with the loft conversion and all. But it's the damage you've done in the family, the loss of trust.'

Tom felt his eyes fill with tears. He bent his head further over, and kicked at the carpet again. 'I've got to be punished, haven't I?'

'You'll punish yourself, lad. It's going to be hard for you to get back to where you were with Davy and Vivien. As for the money, we'll take it out of the sum set aside for your day trip to France.'.

'Which means I can't go?'

'Which means you can't go. I think that's fair, don't you?'

Tom sniffed, richly. It was fair, of course. But it was a bad blow. He'd been looking forward to that, for ages. And the Whistler would be lost without Tom.

Tom thought, if I'd said 'no' to the Whistler, this wouldn't have happened. I ought to have said 'no'. But I wanted to look different from Davy, and I wanted . . . I wanted to show I was on the Whistler's side. I am on his side. I'm not sorry I did it, not one bit!

'Forrester, T,' said Mr Carton. It was the first lesson of the day, and Mr Carton was ticking names off on the register.

'Here, sir,' said Tom, in a bored tone.

Mr Carton glanced up and down. Then he lifted his head again, his eyes sharpening into bayonet points.

'Come here,' he said, pointing to a space in front of his table.

Tom shuffled out, keeping his head high. His ears were red and puffy from the darning needle, and his head felt chilly, but his cockscomb of hair was as stiff as grease could make it.

Mr Carton closed his eyes and covered them with his hand in an exaggerated gesture of despair. 'And what do you think you're playing at?'

'Nothing, sir.'

'That's right, nothing. I'm not having you in my class looking like that. You're a disgrace to the school. I'll give you a note to take to the head of the Lower School. He'll suspend you till you can come to class looking like a normal boy. You understand?'

Tom swallowed hard. He'd half expected it, of course, but it wasn't pleasant. He could hear titters going round the class behind him. The Pakis and Wogs and all that lot would be having a field day at his expense. Tom hated everyone.

He took the note Mr Carton gave him, marched down the corridor to the classroom at the end, endured a blighting comment from the head of the Lower School, and then marched himself out of the main entrance into the street.

A melodious whistling announced that the Whistler was before him.

'Hi,' said the Whistler. 'Thought I'd join you, since it looked a dull sort of day on the timetable.'

'But,' said Tom, 'you've got that lovely poem to give in. You'd get a really good mark for that, maybe an A. And you can't afford to fall behind with your work.'

'Neither can you.'

'If you went back to classes, you could make notes, and give them to me after, so that I didn't lose out. And let me know what homework to do.'

Almost, the Whistler was persuaded. Then he shrugged. 'School's a drag. All for one, and one for all, or something like that. Let's go play games, and make ourselves some money at the same time.'

'I could do with some money,' said Tom, thinking that if he could only repay that five pounds, maybe his family would still allow him to go on the day trip. He said, 'Don't get me wrong, Whistler. I really am glad to see you, even if I know you shouldn't.'

They went to the park, and worked out a game of Shipwreck, seeing how they could leap from one piece of apparatus in the playground to another, touching the ground only now and then.

'I suppose,' said Tom, after a while, 'we could earn some money, offering to walk people's dogs.'

'Looking like you do,' said the Whistler, 'they'd be scared to let their pooches be seen out with you.'

Tom laughed. He felt better now he was out in the open, playing with his friend. 'What do we do, then?'

'We play lookouts. We see how many old ladies we can spot going off to the shops with their shopping bags on wheels. We make a note of where they come from, and what time they went.'

'What good does that do?'

'You'll see; come on!'

The Whistler stationed Tom at one end of a nearby street, while he went to the other. They watched and waited and made notes in their homework books. After about half an hour, they compared notes. Three old ladies had gone out to do their shopping, carefully locking their front doors behind them. No doubt they'd be away for some time.

'Now you keep watch for their return,' said the Whistler. 'Or for anyone snooping, like gas men checking meters and the like. If you see anyone come back, or anything unusual, then you hoot like an owl. Right?'

'Right,' said Tom, full of enthusiasm. 'But what will you be doing?'

The Whistler grinned and vanished up the street. Tom turned round and began watching the road. A milk float drove up, and the milkman gave Tom a look full of suspicion. Suddenly Tom felt uneasy. He hooted like an owl.

'Flipping milkman,' said the Whistler, materialising at Tom's side.

'He's watching us. Do you think we ought to explain about my being suspended from school?'

'Pretend you haven't seen him. We'd best move on to the next street, though, because he's had a good look at us.'

'But we're not doing any harm. . . .'

'Come along!' The Whistler towed Tom into the next street, and now they had to start all over again watching who went out, and which way they went. Tom told himself that he was bored with this game, because he didn't see the point of it. When the Whistler came back to compare notes, Tom suggested that they call it a day.

'Don't be stupid!' said the Whistler, and went up the path to number five. Tom began to get really agitated. He hadn't been able to watch the Whistler in the other road, but now he could see that his friend was poking at the door around about the lock. Tom began to get frightened. He thought, Help, the Bird was right! I don't know how to deal with this! Help, Lord!

Around the corner, as if on cue, came the milk float.

Tom hooted like an owl, and the Whistler came back down the path, trying to look innocent.

Tom said, 'We're not playing this game any more. I don't like it.'

'Why not?' said the Whistler, but he turned and walked out of the road at Tom's side.

'I don't like it, because it could get serious. A game is one thing, but maybe you could get carried away at it, and then bad things could happen.'

'Like picking up some cheap money?'

Tom's jaw hardened. 'Money is never cheap. We'd better earn it, if we want some money.'

'Chicken! Coward!'

'I'm no coward, Whistler. I don't want to have to say "no" to you. I like you the most, really I do. But I can't play that sort of game.'

'Afraid of being caught? Scaredy cat!'

Tom looked straight ahead. 'We have to get this straight, once for all.'

'Goody-goody! I don't know why I bother with you!'

It was hard to be called a goody-goody, especially when Tom felt that he hadn't been particularly good at all. He fought down various hasty replies. He tried to think of something nice but firm to say, and found himself without ideas.

'Well,' said the Whistler, at last, 'I suppose you've been brought up differently. Do you want to come back to the flat with me? Get some chips, watch the telly?'

Tom understood that the Whistler was offering an olive branch. There was no point in going to his own home. There would be time enough to break the news of his suspension to his family, later. 'Yeah, why not!' said Tom.

8

The house was in the dismals. For three days now Tom's mum had been going round with a cold. Dumpling had been wailing on and off through the night with teething troubles, and now Sausage and Davy were complaining of pains in their heads and tummies.

Tom didn't feel particularly bright, either, but he wasn't going to go on about it. He looked across at Davy, who was lying curled up on his bed, and offered to help his brother with his English homework. Davy threw a book at Tom, so Tom walked out. Downstairs the telly and the radio were both blaring away, and he could hear his mum on the phone, while Dumpling wailed to herself in the kitchen. In the old days, noise hadn't bothered him, but today it did.

Tom turned up the stairs to the loft. He opened the first door and discovered Sausage, wrapped up in her duvet, fast asleep on the floor. Her room hadn't been painted yet, but like Vivien, she couldn't wait to get a little privacy. She'd got her radio on, full blast. Tom turned it off, and went out, closing the door softly.

He went into Vivien's room. She was sitting on her stool by the window with her oboe in her hands, but she wasn't playing. She was looking out of the window at the darkening sky. It was raining outside.

Tom hesitated. Viv turned round, saw him and said, 'Have you got my Bible again?'

Tom shrugged. He'd been reading the Bible quite a lot while he'd been off school. Viv's was the only copy in the house, unfortunately. He'd not seen so much of the Whistler, who'd been persuaded to go back to school after that first disastrous day off. Since then Tom had been working hard delivering leaflets and free newspapers. He'd worn through his shoes, but managed to replace the five pounds he'd taken from his mum's purse.

In the reflecting glass of the window, he could see his raggedy cockscomb, and the bristly blonde fuzz around it. That was the trouble with a Mohican haircut, it didn't say stay neat for long.

Viv sighed, and put her oboe away. She said, 'Tom, your ears look awfully red. Shall I put something on them?'

'I don't mind if you do.'

He sat still while she dabbed at his earlobes. His ears had been giving him gyp, but he wasn't the sort to complain.

Viv said, slowly, not sure of her ground, 'You know these are in danger of going septic, Tom. I don't suppose your friend bothered to sterilise the needle, did he?'

Tom knew he hadn't. He didn't blame the Whistler, precisely. Tom knew it was mostly his own fault that his ears had gone wrong.

He said, 'Suppose you take the studs out, Viv. Could you?'

Viv took them out. Tom squinched up his eyes and tried to pretend it hadn't hurt. Viv looked a bit white, when she'd finished.

Tom said, 'You're a brave girl, Viv. Mum couldn't have done that without crying.'

'I wasn't very kind to you about the money. And when you came to me for help, I wasn't at all nice to you.'

Tom said, making a big concession, 'I ought not to have sung out of tune when your choirmistress gave me that audition.'

'Would you try again?'

'I don't know. It's not really what I want.'

'What do you really want, then?'

'To be friends with the Whistler, but to be able to say "no". How do I do that, Viv?'

Viv sat down and looked at him. She looked for a long time. For a moment or two she looked as wise as the Bird. She said, 'You know, Tom, you needn't worry about looking like Davy, any more. You're growing up faster than him, I suppose. Your nose and chin stick out more, and you look as if you do a lot of thinking.'

'Thank you, sis.' Tom gave her a jerky bow.

'Are you bored, being at home?'

No one else had thought he might be bored. Not even his mum.

'Yes, but I can't go back, looking like this.'

'I could cut your hair, and we could try smarming it down with grease. I'm sure Mr Carton would pass it, if he sees you'd tried to look normal.'

'I don't mind,' said Tom. 'But Viv, will you help me with the other thing? How do I say "no" to the Whistler?'

'I've been thinking about it a lot,' said Vivien. 'I think you've got to pray for help, to make you strong. God always listens to the prayers of those who believe in him.'

'Even those doubting Thomases like me?'

'I think everyone has doubts now and then. But if you pray hard, the doubts go away.'

'Do you believe, really truly, all the time?'

Viv hesitated. 'I've only started to believe recently. But I tell you this, Tom. It works. It really works. Christ did die for us, and we only have to believe that, to be saved. If he did that for us, he won't leave us in the lurch when we ask him for help. You ought to talk to someone who knows more than me.'

'You've helped me a lot, Viv. Now let's see if Mum will let us borrow her cutting-out shears, so that I can get my hair cut.'

Vivien cut Tom's hair, they smarmed it down, and though it looked a bit odd, Mr Carton didn't say anything when Tom reported for school next day. Davy didn't make it to school, because he was still in bed, clutching his tummy. The Whistler didn't look quite as pleased to see his friend as Tom had expected. The Whistler had gone back to mixing with his old pals and Bongo, while Tom had been away.

'There's a plot afoot,' said the Whistler to Tom, in the dinner hour. 'You want to come in on it? It's going to be ace!'

'What? When?' Tom was getting cautious about the Whistler's ideas, especially if they had originated in the brains of the Whistler's old pals.

'Can't tell you now,' said the Whistler, as one of the teachers passed nearby. 'I'll tell you when we get on the boat to France.'

'I can't come. Remember?'

'I'd forgotten.'

'I doubt if Davy will make it, either. He's got the collywobbles, and the last thing he wants is to be tossed up and down in a ship for hours.'

'Take his place, then,' said the ever-practical Whistler.

Tom was silent. Part of him said that was a brilliant idea, but another part advised caution.

'I'll have to ask me mum,' said Tom, thinking that she'd probably say 'No'. His mum was in a bit of a state, what with Davy and Sausage and the Dumpling all being sick at once. She'd probably do her barmy, if he asked her for a favour.

'You'll know how to get round her,' said the Whistler.

Tom did know how. That evening he was so helpful to his mother that she wondered if he were sickening for something, too. He washed up, and remembered to hang up the tea towels instead of wadding them into a bundle on the floor. He picked up all Dumpling's toys from the floor and he hoovered the carpet. He even took Viv to and from choir practice without grumbling. At the same time, Tom did a little praying on the side.

He wasn't absolutely sure that he ought to pray for his brother to go on being ill, but he did pray that if Davy were going to continue sick, that he, Tom, might take Davy's place.

He also began, humbly, to ask forgiveness for his stupid, thoughtless sins. He prayed for help and strength. And he prayed for the Whistler. Oh, how he prayed for the Whistler! He was tired out when he'd finished praying for the Whistler. He even spared a prayer for poor, silly Bongo, who would surely get into trouble on the French trip if given half a chance.

It sounded as if mischief were afoot, and if mischief were afoot then the Whistler and Bongo were bound to get mixed up in it. Tom prayed that God would give him strength to rescue his friends from evil, if it happened; though of course he also prayed rather hard that it wouldn't happen.

In the morning Davy was better, but very white and

sleepy. Tom's mother listened to his request, and gave permission for him to go in Davy's place. She said she'd give him a note to give to the teachers about it, but then Dumpling was sick all over the kitchen floor, so Tom went off without the note.

He smarmed down his hair, and for once he tried to look as much like Davy as possible. He had to be early at the school gates, to get on the coach. When he got there, the master in charge called out his name, 'Forrester', just like that. The master didn't say Forrester D, or anything. He just said Forrester. So Tom said 'Here, sir', and climbed up into the coach to find a seat beside the Whistler and Bongo.

'Got any bread?' said Bongo, with a mysterious air.

'Bread? Oh, money,' said Tom. 'Yes, I offered my mum the money I'd earned last week, but she said to keep it, to spend in France. She said to spend it on myself and not on presents for the family, but they've been so decent I'll try to get them all something.'

'Oh, we'll find something to spend it on,' said the Whistler, looking sly.

'What's the plan, then?' said Tom.

'I'll tell you later.'

Two boys came down the aisle of the coach towards them. They were very large. Tom knew they had been at the Whistler's old school, and he had heard that they had been at the bottom of a lot of bullying of new boys this year. They weren't in Mr Carton's form, and Tom was glad about that, for he didn't like them.

The larger of the boys looked at Tom, but spoke to the Whistler. 'Who's he?'

'He's my friend,' said the Whistler, and Tom understood by the conciliatory way that the Whistler spoke, that it was wise to walk warily with these two boys.

'Is he all right?' said the bully boy.

'Sure,' said the Whistler. 'He's been out with me, playing games. He makes a good look-out.'

The two boys went off, swaggering.

'Now, look!' said Tom. 'If there's any funny business like that game you got me into . . .'

'There isn't.'

'I'm not going to get mixed up in anything criminal.'

'You won't,' said the Whistler, and gave a jaunty laugh.

Tom wasn't as satisfied as he ought to have been by this assurance, but he let it go for now. The coach was travelling fast and furious down the motorway. Soon they would be at Dover, and then they would get off the coach and take their first ever sea trip. It was exciting.

Bongo yawned. They'd all had to get up early, to catch the coach.

The Whistler said, 'The English teacher did give me an A for that poem about the kite, and he says he wants to put it in the school magazine.'

Tom grinned, thrilled for his friend. The Whistler tried to look as if getting an A was something that happened to him every week, but he couldn't quite make it.

'Fame at last,' said Tom, ribbing him.

'Yeah.' The Whistler's face clouded over. 'Me dad will be out before Christmas, he says.'

This wasn't particularly good news. By now Tom had a pretty good idea of what went on in the Whistler's home, and his admiration for his friend's courage had grown accordingly.

The Whistler's mum worked as an office cleaner in the early mornings and in the evenings. During the day she looked after her daughter's toddler, who was spoilt rotten one moment, and whacked for crying the next.

The Whistler's much older sister had divorced her husband and come back to live with her mother, but had lately allowed her boyfriend to move into her bedroom in the flat, while the toddler was shoved out into the sitting-room.

The Whistler also slept in the sitting-room, on a pull-out bed. There were only two bedrooms in the flat, one for his mum, and one for his sister. His sister worked in a supermarket during the day, and spent her evenings at the disco.

'What about getting re-housed?' said Tom. 'My dad says you'd have enough points, especially when your dad's home again.'

'My mum tried, down at the Council. But she's so tired all the time, she's lost heart.'

'You haven't, though. Why don't you go with her?'

Tom could see the Whistler turning that over in his mind. Maybe he'd do it, at that.

'One good thing about dad coming home,' said the Whistler, brightening, 'is that he'll throw me sister's boyfriend out, 'cause my dad doesn't approve of mixing with coloureds, and my sister's boyfriend is a Paki.'

'Oh, they're all right,' said Tom.

'Flipping Pakis,' said the Whistler, and he smiled in a not nice way.

There were a whole group of Pakis and Sikhs at the front of the coach, all squealing at their first sight of the sea. Many of them had been born in England, but had never seen the sea before.

Neither had the Whistler, though he tried not to show that he was impressed. Tom and his family always went to the seaside every year, living in a rented cottage, so he knew all about the sea. But Tom had never been on a large boat before. Except for a few excited remarks, the party of schoolchildren fell silent as they got off their coach and trailed after the teachers up this way and down that till they finally stepped on board the ferry.

'Now take care not to get lost,' said the teacher in charge. 'There are dozens of other school parties on this trip with you. We'll all go together to one of the big lounges, and then if you want to explore you may, provided you get back to us safely, half an hour before we're due to dock in France. Understood?'

9

The Whistler was so excited his eyes shone black in a white face. His eyes weren't really black, but they looked it in the dull light between decks.

'Let's go right down to the bottom, and work our way up, exploring.'

Tom caught Bongo's arm. 'Are you coming?'

Bongo shook him off, and lumbered over to a distant corner of the vast lounge, where there was a row of games machines.

'Let him go,' said the Whistler, impatiently. 'He can't come to much harm.'

'He'll spend all his money before he gets to France.'

'There is that.' The Whistler had a word with Bongo, who was agreeable to giving most of his cash into his friend's safe-keeping.

Then Tom and the Whistler raced down and around and down again, till they got quite dizzy and hadn't a clue which way up they were. They discovered the coaches and cars, neatly stored away on the lowest level. They found arcades of duty-free shops selling all sorts of enticing goodies. They saw more and more games machines, and restaurants and bars; and at last they found themselves back in their own big lounge.

But there was no one from their own party there. They wandered around, feeling strange. Soon they would dock in France, and what would become of them if they couldn't find their own coach party?

Then Tom saw a sign saying that you could get foreign exchange on the next deck. He remembered that he'd got to get some French money, and he also remembered that the bank was right at the end of the lounge in which they were supposed to meet their party. There wasn't just one lounge, but two.

So they tore back up the stairs and there they found the rest of their party, all getting anxious about them. Bongo had lost all the money he'd retained, so it was a good thing the Whistler had kept some back for him.

They docked at Boulogne and traipsed off, going this way and that till they connected with their coach again.

'Now,' said the master in charge. 'We're going straight to a hypermarket on the outskirts of the town. You'll find a lot of interesting things to buy there, at all sorts of prices. I won't tell you to spend your money wisely, because I don't suppose you'd listen . . .'

There were ironic cheers at that, and the master smiled.

'. . . but do remember what you were told yesterday in Assembly. No booze, please. You will have just over an hour at the hypermarket, and then we will go into Boulogne itself where you can eat your sandwiches, or try your French out in a cafe or shop, or just wander around till it's time for the return journey. Good luck.'

They cheered him again, because he'd smiled when he'd told them to behave, and then they all piled off and ran into the hypermarket. This was a vast place, with wide corridors between the different sections. It was much bigger than any supermarket Tom and the Whistler had ever seen, and it sold a much greater variety of things.

There were foodstuffs which neither of them had ever seen before, and didn't know if they'd like, either. There were banks of toiletries which the Whistler said his sister would do her barmy over, and there were ornaments and knick-knacks with French names on them which might be nice to take home for the family, or might not, depending on the price.

'Look at those shirts!' said the Whistler, pointing to a gaudy row of clothes. Neither of the boys would be seen dead in anything like that.

'Now this is more like,' said the Whistler, fingering some beautifully made penknives. 'I've always wanted a really sharp knife.'

'I did have a small penknife once,' said Tom, 'but Davy lost it down a grating in the road. I must say, these do look good.'

The Whistler was fiddling around with a wicked-looking blade. It was a flick knife. He saw Tom looking at him and said, 'Well, why not? It would be quite safe to carry in my pocket.'

Tom wasn't sure why not, but he felt, obscurely, that a flick knife wasn't the happiest choice to make. Tom hesitated for a long time over the penknives, and meanwhile the Whistler wandered away to another section.

Tom thought that if he did buy himself a good knife, he could still afford to get the family some croissants, fresh ones, in Boulogne. He thought they wouldn't really mind if he bought himself something for a change. His mother had said he should.

By the time Tom had paid for the knife, the Whistler and Bongo were nowhere to be seen. Tom tore to the end of the long corridor he was in, and there they were coming towards him, laughing, carrying bulky plastic bags.

Tom looked at what was sticking out of the top of those bags, and felt his stomach contract.

'What have you got there? Booze?'

'What's it to you?' said Bongo, quick enough for once.

'Just mineral water,' said the Whistler, but he looked away as he said it.

'If it is booze,' began Tom.

'No business of yours if it is,' said the Whistler. 'You'll be glad enough of a mouthful when we're on the boat going back. Especially if the sea is rough.'

'We're going to have fun on the way back,' said Bongo, nodding.

Tom was beginning to get a nasty sick feeling in the pit of his stomach. Of course, it might be that he was going down with the family tummy bug, but on the other hand it might be something quite different.

If there was any mischief about, he knew who would be in it, up to his neck. In Assembly the previous day, they'd been warned against buying liquor of any kind. Or offensive weapons. Tom hadn't understood why, not properly. Now he was beginning to understand, and he didn't like it. Tom thought about telling one of the teachers that the Whistler and Bongo had bought some booze. He decided against it. He couldn't rat on them. Besides, as the Whistler had said, what harm could it do?

The Whistler took off his sweater and arranged it over the bottles in his carrier bag, so that the masters shouldn't see what he'd bought, as they trooped back into the coach. They drove into Boulogne itself. There they all piled out, and the teachers said they could go where they liked and do what they liked, provided they were back at the coach in two hours' time, when they would be starting back for the boat.

The Whistler, Bongo and Tom got away from the busy streets which looked like the streets of a busy town, anywhere. They walked down a side street in search of a delicatessen where they could buy some food. Neither the Whistler nor Bongo had been able to get their mothers organised enough to put them up a packed lunch like everyone else, and though Tom had scrounged some slices of bread and a hunk of cheese, it wasn't going to see three of them through that long day. Tom tried out his French in a delicatessen, and apart from getting confused as to which of the succulent.sausages he wanted sliced up for them, they got on fairly well. They bought some fruit at an outdoor stall, and went to sit on some steps while they ate.

They sat there, talking about this and that, for quite a while. It was different in France. The traffic was different, and the smells and the sounds of everyday life were different. Tom wanted to soak it all up, and he could see the Whistler's eyes going this way and that, recording the scene in his memory banks. The Whistler was bright. Maybe he could make a new poem out of this. In his old school he'd tried not to appear brighter than his mates, because he'd needed to be part of a group.

In Tom's old school, he and Davy had spent a lot of time thinking up mischief, because they could usually cotton on to what the teacher said quickly, which left a lot of spare time for thinking up things to do after school.

In their new school, neither Tom nor the Whistler were allowed to sit back and be lazy. They felt new horizons opening before them. The Whistler said he was going to start keeping a notebook, to write down odd thoughts that occurred to him. Tom thought he might well do the same. Maybe they'd write a new poem together, or a play, even.

Presently Bongo, who had wandered away by himself, returned with a carrier bag, looking smug.

'What have you got there?' asked Tom.

'Bangers and matches.'

Tom thought Bongo had said 'Bangers and mash'. He thought Bongo had made a joke, and he laughed. The Whistler didn't laugh, but he did frown and say it might be a good idea to walk around a bit.

They went and bought some croissants for Tom's mum, and they lingered in a newsagents, trying to work out the headlines in the French newspapers.

They decided they'd be grand and lordly, and have a black coffee each in a cafe, and then it was time to get back to the coach.

They climbed back into the coach and collapsed. It wasn't that it was late in the day, but that they'd seen a lot and done a lot of new things. Time to be quiet.

The coach was relatively silent on the way back to the boat. Tom dozed off. When he woke up, the Whistler was missing. Looking around for his friend, Tom was disturbed to see the Whistler with his head close to that of one of the Bully Boys. Both were glancing forward up the coach to where the coloured boys and girls were sitting.

Tom felt uneasiness settle into his stomach, and stay there.

When the Whistler came back to his seat, Tom asked him what was up.

'I'll tell you on the boat.'

They piled off the coach and trailed up onto the boat. It was not the same boat as before, but a slightly older, not so smartly painted boat. But it was just as big, if not bigger. Tom could see that they were just as likely to get lost on this boat as they had on the earlier one. He stuck close to the Whistler, who was looking this way and that, with narrowed eyes.

'What's up?' said Tom.

The Whistler drew Tom aside. They were in one of the big lounges. The teachers had thrown themselves down and looked set to stay there. The coloured boys and girls were streaming off in search of games machines. The Bully Boys were sitting together in a tight group, doing nothing, not talking, watching the coloured boys and girls.

'We're going to have some fun with the Pakis,' said the Whistler.

Tom felt a shot of bile hit the back of his mouth. This was the moment of truth. This was the moment when he had to say "no" to the Whistler. Tom tried to get the word out, and failed.

'Are you all right?' said the Whistler, looking anxious. 'You've gone a funny colour.'

'I'm all right. It's you who are all wrong. You can't mean what I thought you said, Whistler.'

The Whistler looked disconcerted for a moment, and then rallied. 'Of course I mean it. We're going to wait till they go down to the loos and then we're going to pile in and have some fun with them. That'll learn them not to walk so high and mighty.'

'Now wait a minute,' said Tom, trying to keep calm. 'They are as British as you and me. They have every right to be here. And they're not really cocky. They just work hard, that's all.'

'I work hard, too,' said the Whistler, looking dangerous. 'And I know I don't have a chance of getting a job when I leave school, because of them.'

'That's nonsense and you know it. Whistler, use your head! This isn't your sort of scene any more.'

'Yes, it is. My old mates asked me if I were going in with them, and I said yes. I told them you were all right, too. So shut up, and get your knife ready.'

'Knife?' said Tom, taking a step back. 'The penknife I bought?'

'Didn't you buy a flick knife? I did.'

The Whistler pulled out his flick knife, pressed the catch, and a long, wicked-looking blade sprang out.

Tom thought, Lord, help!

He said, 'No!'

10

'What do you mean, "No"?' said the Whistler.

'No,' said Tom, in a firmer voice. 'I can't do this, Whistler, and I don't want you to do it, either.'

'No one's going to split on us, if that's what you're afraid of.'

'You mean it's all right, if no one finds out?'

The Whistler looked as if he'd like to hit Tom, if it were worth it.

Tom said, 'Think, Whistler. Think about what you're planning to do! This wasn't your idea, was it?'

'Well, no. But . . .'

'I know you did have some stupid ideas about coloured people when we first met, but I thought you'd come to see that was all wrong, and to live and let live.'

'Maybe I did think of laying off them for a while, but . . .'

'It's the Bully Boys from your old school who've thought this up, isn't it? Whistler, you can't do this! It's awful!'

The Whistler hunched his shoulders. 'What's so awful about a bit of pushing and shoving?'

'With knives? Suppose you did a bit of pushing and shoving with a knife . . .'

'The knives are only to frighten. If they stand still, no one will get hurt.'

'They'd only be roughed up a bit, is that it? Do you think it would be a fair fight?'

'Fair enough. There's enough of them rotten Pakis around to sink a battleship.'

'Then you've got to work that much harder. Whistler, please! Stop and think!'

'I have thought.' His tone was sullen, and he avoided Tom's eye.

Tom tried again. 'Look, are you going into this because you're afraid of your old friends? Fine friends they are, dragging you into this sort of thing! Suppose someone was killed.'

'That's stupid!'

'It could happen, with knives, couldn't it?'

'Look, all we're going to do is let off a few fireworks to make them squeal, and then I'll cover them with my knife while my friends. . . .'

'. . . beat them up? Those undersized kids? Girls and all? Your old friends are roughly twice the size of most of the Pakis. Is that fair?'

The Whistler turned and walked away, hands in pockets. Tom hesitated, and then went after him.

'Whistler!'

'I thought you were my friend!'

'I am, and that's why . . .'

'Goody-goody. I suppose you're going to split on us to the teachers!'

'No, because you're going to stop it, Whistler.'

'You must be joking!' The Whistler shook Tom off, and went to join the Bully Boys. Tom watched. In a moment, the Whistler and one of the bigger boys got bottles out of their bags, and they all began to drink. Soon they were laughing loudly in that group.

Tom ran away.

The boat was crowded not only with schoolchildren but also with families on shopping sprees. Everywhere Tom looked there were people shouting, talking, laughing. You couldn't move for kids running around.

Tom went down and down into the bottom of the boat. He hadn't any particular plan in mind. He just wanted to get away and hide.

Only there wasn't anywhere in that whole vast, floating world, in which you could hide.

He arrived at a bank of loos and went in. Kids were coming and going in all directions, banging doors, splashing, arguing. Adults were pushing and shoving. There was a queue.

Tom suddenly found he simply couldn't wait for his turn. He needed to get in there, quick. He dived into one by itself on the end, which had a notice on it saying 'Out of Order'. It was clean, and there was paper in it. He thought the flush probably wouldn't work but it did.

He didn't move, when he'd finished. He sat there, arguing with God. Tom told God that the odds were too high. Tom said he couldn't sneak. Even if he did sneak, he'd lose his friend, which would be bad enough, but worse still, the Whistler would probably be suspended from school and that might tip him right over the edge into Badland.

God didn't say anything. At least, Tom didn't hear him saying anything. Perhaps because Tom was doing all the talking, and doing his best not to listen to anything God might be saying to him.

When Tom had tired himself out, he stopped arguing.

Immediately he remembered something that he'd been trying to shut out. Last night Viv had come into his room in her nightdress, and had sat on the edge of his bed. Davy was already asleep.

Viv had said there'd been something on her mind all day. In church the previous Sunday the vicar had asked them, 'Am I my brother's keeper?' He'd told them the story of Cain and Abel from the Old Testament, and then he'd told them that we had a responsibility for one another, that we were all brothers before God.

Viv said that the story had got stuck in her mind, because it reminded her of Tom and the Whistler. Viv said that one part of her didn't want Tom to have anything to do with the Whistler, but the other part said that Tom ought to stick to his friend like glue, to try to keep him straight. Then Viv had gone away. She'd said she'd think about Tom next day, and Tom knew that although Viv had been too shy to say so, she'd meant she was going to pray for him.

He didn't half need her prayers!

By now Tom was limp with worry. Apparently God had won the argument, and Tom had lost. Tom had now got it clear in his mind that he had got to keep on trying with the Whistler, no matter what. And he'd also got to protect the Pakis, who were his brothers, as well. And keep Bongo out of trouble.

It was, he felt, a tall order for one small boy.

Tom got off the loo, sighing heavily. He didn't know what he was going to do, or how he was going to do it, but he supposed he wouldn't get far, sitting on the loo.

He tried to pull back the bolt. It stuck. He tugged at it, and it wobbled in his hands.

So that's why the loo was out of order! If Tom had been that little bit more forceful, the knob would have come right away from the bolt, and he'd have been stuck in the loo until someone could get him out.

Tom stopped to think.

Then he took out his felt-tip pen, and wrote something on the nice clean wall of the loo. He wasn't sure that he was doing the right thing, but with a bit of luck, and a bit of help from his friends – especially the One Above – it might work.

'Well, Lord,' he said, putting the pen away, 'I'll do my bit, but you've got to do your bit, too. "The gang of evil men is around me. Like a pack of dogs they close in on me. Lord, come quickly to my aid."'

He eased back the bolt with care, let himself out into the corridor, and shut the door, leaving the 'Out of Order' sign in place. Then he tramped and climbed steadily up through the boat until he located the Bully Boys, Whistler and Bongo. They were all very merry by now, somewhat bleary eyed and loud voiced.

Tom stood on the edge of the group, and beckoned to the Whistler.

'What is it, then?' said the Whistler, swaggering over to Tom.

Tom lowered his voice. 'I wrote part of your poem in one of the loos, and put an "Out of Order" sign on the door. Want to see?'

Who could resist? Not the Whistler. He told his friends that he wouldn't be a tick, and went down to the loos with Tom. The 'Out of Order' sign was still in place.

'I dare you to write in the rest of your poem,' said Tom. 'I only got the first line down. But you'll have to shoot the lock hard when you get in, because it sticks, and you don't want anyone disturbing you.'

The Whistler went into the loo, shot the bolt home,

and laughed out loud when he saw what Tom had written. Fame at last! This would be even better than having his poem printed in the school magazine, because in the loos lots of people would read it, and wonder who'd written it.

Tom stood outside, waiting and praying.

'Lord, help me. Help the Whistler. He's not bad, really. He's on a knife edge, torn between good and bad. Please help him, and please don't let the Pakis get beaten up, and please don't let poor silly Bongo get into trouble.'

'Hey!' said the Whistler, rattling the door. 'The knob's come off. Hey, Tom! I can't get out. Tom, are you there?'

'Yes,' said Tom. 'I'll go and get someone.'

The Whistler's voice changed. 'You knew! It was a trick!'

'Yes. You'll be safe there, Whistler. I'll see if I can get Bongo down here, too.'

Whistler rattled the door, and kicked it. 'You flipping well let me out! Now!'

'I can't. I don't know how.'

There was silence. Heavy breathing.

'Tom, if you don't let me out, you'll be sorry, I swear it!'

'Yes, I know. But I'd be sorrier if you'd gone ahead with your plan. Now you've got a perfect alibi, so keep quiet, and I'll fetch help.'

Tom tore off back up the stairs, going dizzily round and round. He found the lounge in which he'd left the others. But they weren't there. Maybe he'd got lost, as had happened before. He told himself to stop and think.

'Help, Lord,' he prayed. 'Which way do I go? What do I do? Do I try to tell the teachers, and would they believe me?'

Then he saw one of the Pakis going round the corner

away from him, into a small amusement arcade. Tom followed. Yes, there were all the coloured boys and girls from his school.

Tom had never been particularly friendly with them, nor they with him. He took a deep breath, steadied himself, and stepped in amongst them.

'Hi!' he said. 'Listen, you're in danger here. Could you come out into the main lounge, where everyone can see you?'

'What for? Who? What did he say?'

'He's one of them. He's with the Whistler!'

'No,' said Tom, trying to keep calm. 'I am with the Whistler, but he's out of it. The Bully Boys have some sort of plan on. At least, that's what I heard. And maybe Bongo as well. With fireworks, and maybe with knives. If you all come out of this confined space, and sit down in the open lounge, I don't think anyone can touch you.'

'Fireworks? Don't be daft!'

'Bangers and matches,' said Tom, holding his ground. 'I thought Bongo said he'd bought bangers and mash, but he didn't. He's bought firecrackers. Jumping jacks, and a box of matches. Please come out of here, all of you!'

'Why should you care?'

Tom thought, I don't, not really. These aren't my brothers, not like the Whistler. Why should I get myself banged about for this lot?

But clear as a bell inside his head, he heard Viv's distressed voice saying, "Everyone is your brother, in a way".

Tom swallowed hard. 'It's because it's not fair. Because God said so.'

Someone said, 'Why, he's a something Christian!'

'Yes,' said Tom, 'It's because I'm a Christian. Now will you all come out of there, fast?'

They began to move out, but as they did so, Bongo appeared and threw something into their midst. It went off with a bang. The girls screamed, and so did some of the boys. The Bully Boys rushed in, with their big bovver boots, stamping and kicking. Chairs were knocked over and Tom caught a glimpse of a wicked-looking knife in someone's hand.

Tom went for the boy who was holding the knife, even though the lad was nearly twice Tom's size. The next few minutes were confused. Tom felt himself being picked up, and then thrown roughly aside. He got up again, feeling dizzy. A brown hand pulled him out of the way of a rush by the Bully Boys, but Tom's shoulder was caught, and he was whirled round and down again. He tried to get up, but someone was leaning on him. A pair of brown legs was in front of him, and Tom could see that there was a scrimmage going on, from where he lay on the ground.

The brown legs in front of him were swept away. Somebody else fell over Tom, and winded him all over again. More firecrackers went off, there were some more screams, and then some heavier voices joined in the noise.

Breathing hard, Tom was dragged to his feet, and shaken by a large adult.

'He was trying to help us!' cried one of the brown-skinned girls. 'He came to warn us! Yes, he's all right, he is!'

'Forrester?' said a voice above Tom's head. 'Are you in with this shower or not?'

Tom felt rather tired, and somewhat sick. He managed to say he was trying to stop the fighting, and then he sat down in a corner, very thankful that it was all over. The masters were sorting out the Bully Boys. A woman who said she knew first aid helped with a couple of minor injuries. Tom's shoulder ached, and so did one of his legs.

There were a lot of questions being asked, but luckily no

one seemed to want to know exactly how Tom had heard about the plan to rough up the Pakis. Tom kept in the background as much as he could. He heard one of the masters explaining to someone who looked official, that there had been a bit of a rough-house, but that it was all over now. Then someone else came along and said they'd best collect their belongings, as they'd be docking any minute.

Tom remembered the Whistler. He got himself to his feet with an effort, and said he had to go to the loo. He dragged himself down to the loos, and banged on the door which still said 'Out of Order'.

'You still there, Whistler? It's all over. You can come out now.'

'How can I?' said the Whistler, vibrating with rage.

'Stick the point of your new knife into the hole where the knob went in, and I think you'll be able to move the bolt back.'

The Whistler scrabbled around, got the bolt drawn back, and stepped out. He looked hard at Tom, who was somewhat the worse for wear.

'They fought, the masters separated them. Lots of questions were asked, but no one mentioned your name. We're docking in a minute.'

Tom hoped the Whistler would shake hands, or thank him, but he didn't. Instead, he said, 'I don't believe you. You must have ratted on us!' He stalked off, head in the air. Tom thought, I'm surprised the Whistler didn't think of that trick with the knife himself. Maybe he did. Maybe God was having an argument with him, too. Maybe the Whistler was pleased, really, that he couldn't get out.

They trailed off the boat, and got into the coach. The Whistler went to sit with his old friends, and ignored Tom. Tom felt bad about that.

Then their coach, instead of going straight through Customs, was directed into a special area. Everyone was told to get off. They had to go into a waiting-room, where they were to be searched.

'Someone,' said one of the Bully Boys loudly, 'has split on us!'

11

It was trouble, all right. Everyone looked at Tom.

'I didn't split,' said Tom wearily. 'What do you expect, if you flash knives and drink around on the boat? Did you think no one would notice?'

The coach was searched. All the seats were pulled apart.

All the passengers were searched, and some were taken away into another room for questioning. The Bully Boys were away a long time, and so was poor old Bongo.

The rest sat, or lay around, too tired to be angry. Most were anxious, because time was creeping on, and soon their parents would be arriving at the school to pick them up . . . and they wouldn't be there. The masters were in a tearing temper because what had happened reflected on them. Everyone was edgy. Two of the girls cried because they were scared and it was getting late and they were a long way from home.

Rumours circulated. It was said that the coach driver had shopped them because he wouldn't take his coach out with a load of boys carrying flick knives and firecrackers on board. Someone else said the Customs people had been tipped off that their coach was carrying drugs.

Tom wouldn't have minded the delay, if only the Whistler hadn't been giving him the cold shoulder as well. The Whistler sat by himself, looking pinched and white.

They didn't get back to the school until just before midnight, and as they got down from the coach, the Whistler brushed past Tom and said, 'You wait! Me and my friends are going to get you for this!'

Tom trudged along at Vivien's side on the way to choir practice. Tom hadn't seen or heard anything from the Whistler over the weekend, and there had been no sign of him at school that day. There hadn't been any sign of the Bully Boys, either. Rumour had it that they'd been suspended, as had poor, silly Bongo.

Viv said, 'Cheer up. You'll soon make more friends.'

Tom didn't reply. He was in a black mood.

He saw Viv into the vestry where they were having choir practice, and then went to sit at the back of the church to get away from the row. He got out his homework books, but he couldn't concentrate. He felt as flat as a pancake.

The church door opened a little way, and someone whistled to him.

Tom lifted his head. He didn't think that was the Whistler signalling to him, because the way the Whistler made music, you'd think it was a blackbird calling from the top of a tree. This was a hoarse sort of whistle, more of a croak. But who else would whistle to Tom? Perhaps the Whistler had a bad throat, and that's why he'd been off school that day.

Tom went to the door to see who it was. A large hand seized his arm, and pulled him outside. They were standing in a dark forecourt, a little to one side of the main body of the church.

87

Four large dark figures loomed over Tom.

Tom swallowed. The Bully Boys had arrived to exact retribution.

It wasn't any use telling them that he hadn't sneaked on them. They didn't want to believe it. They were angry because he'd tried to upset their plans, and now they were going to take it out of him. Tom looked around for the Whistler and Bongo, but they weren't there. Tom supposed that was something to be thankful for.

He tried to back up against the wall, but the big lad who was holding his arm, wouldn't let him.

Tom prayed, 'My enemies surround me. Oh Lord, come quickly to my rescue!'

Tom felt as if someone or something had bubbled up inside him, giving him courage. He felt, suddenly, not at all afraid. He felt as if he'd grown six inches and could cope with anything.

Four against one. Big odds.

'Kick him to pieces!'

As the four lads moved in on Tom, around the corner came two figures, one small and slim, and the other blundering along.

'You leave him alone!' yelled the Whistler. 'He's my friend, and I won't have him done over!'

One of the large lads swept back his right arm, casually, and knocked the Whistler off his feet.

Bongo skidded to a halt, looking dazed.

'Off!' The biggest lad jerked a thumb at Bongo, who stopped and stared, looking now at the winded Whistler, and now at Tom.

'Grab him!' Tom's arm was twisted up and behind him. He lashed out with his free arm, all the time hoping, praying, praying . . .

Would Viv hear him, if he screamed for help?

'Whoops-a-daisy!' A strange voice, and a stranger accent. The big lads fell away from Tom like nine-pins knocked over by a well-aimed ball.

'Careful does it!' The bully boy who had been gripping Tom's arm released his hold with a yell of pain.

Tom opened his eyes wide. Four vanquished bully boys lay around the forecourt. The Whistler was being pulled to his feet. Bongo had vanished.

Five boys and two girls of about Tom's age were standing in a bunch by the door to the church hall at the end of the forecourt. A tall athletic man in a track suit was dusting himself down.

'Judo, black belt,' he said, in a broad Northern accent. He smiled at Tom. 'Comes in useful, sometimes. You're the brother of the new girl in the choir, aren't you? She said you might like to join us in the Youth Club some time. She said to keep an eye out for you. Come on in, and meet the boys and girls, and tell us all about it.'

Tom looked around for the Whistler, only to see him disappear into the darkness. He thought for a moment, and then followed his rescuer into the church hall.

Mr Bird called Tom into his room after school next day.

'Tell me about it,' said Mr Bird.

Tom sighed. He'd hoped to catch up with the Whistler after school today, but there was no chance of that, if the Bird wanted a talk. The Whistler had reappeared in school, looking pale, and avoiding Tom. The sooner they had it out, the better.

Meanwhile, he had to give the Bird his side of the story.

'I see,' said the Bird, when Tom had finished. 'I

89

suppose you've heard that the police are taking proceedings against four of our ex-pupils?'

'Not against Bongo, sir? He wasn't at school today.'

'No, but he's suspended for a week. With regard to your friend, the Whistler,' and here the Bird pushed one side of his face about till it looked as if he were winking at Tom. 'I gather you've learned to say "no"?'

'Yessir.' He thought, And lost my friend in doing so.

'You did well. I rather think the school is going to be proud of you, Tom. You had me worried, a while back. Shaving your head and truanting, it put a certain label on you which signalled danger to me. I'm glad that label turned out to be misleading.'

Tom said, 'I suppose I was in danger for a while. But I want to wear another label in future.'

The Bird nodded. '"By their works you shall know them." Yes, Tom. I understand that you want to wear the label of a Christian, in future. The word has gone round the school. A lot of people who've never even set eyes on you, have been talking about the boy who said "no".'

Tom looked at the cross on the wall behind the Bird, and wondered if he could get one like it. Would Davy object? Would it matter if he did?

But the Bird was still talking. 'Sometimes, Tom, I get depressed about the state of the world. I feel a sense of failure because four bad lads have to be expelled from this school. But then I see you pulling through, and pulling the Whistler and maybe even Bongo after you. . . . well. . . .'

He shook Tom's hand, man to man.

'Go on,' said the Bird, still smiling. 'Your friend's waiting for you outside.'

Tom cocked an ear, and heard it, too. Someone was whistling sweet and low outside the Bird's window.

90

Tom ran out. He felt marvellous. He grinned at the Whistler, and punched him on the shoulder, lightly.

The Whistler punched him back. 'What are you doing tonight?'

Suddenly Tom saw the way clear before him. 'We're going to pick up Bongo, and take him down to the Youth Club. They asked for volunteers to collect junk for their bonfire. They're going to have a big fireworks display on Guy Fawkes night, and we're to sell hot dogs and coke and soup and coffee. But first we've got to get crates, and old tyres, anything that will burn.'

'I'm not coming to no Youth Club.'

'Aren't you?' Tom smiled. He knew he was on a winning streak.

The Whistler's shoulders jerked up and down. 'I know where there's some bits of broken furniture you could have. Back of the shops in the Lane. They threw them out for the dustmen to take, but the dustmen left them, and no one would know if you took them instead.'

'We have to ask permission. Suppose you and Bongo and I go along and ask, all together.'

'I'm not coming to no Youth Club.'

'Yes, you are. And Bongo, too. You're coming because it'll be fun, and because it will keep Bongo off the streets.'

'I'm not coming to no. . . .'

'You can come back to our place for tea first, if you like. Mum says she doesn't mind if we have friends in to tea, so long as we do the clearing up, after. You can wash, I'll dry.'

'What, me do the washing up? You have got a screw loose!'

Tom laughed. He took the turning down to his road, striding out in a marching style. He began to whistle one

91

of his friend's favourite tunes. Half way down the road he began to worry, in case the Whistler wasn't following him. He slowed down, and looked back over his shoulder. The Whistler was drifting along some way behind, looking as if he'd taken that turning off the main road by accident.

Tom sent up a quick vote of thanks, and switched to a song he'd heard them practising in church the other night.

> 'Fight the good fight with all thy might,
>   Christ is thy strength, and Christ thy right;
>   Lay hold on life, and it shall be
>   Thy joy and crown eternally.'

If you have enjoyed this Leopard Book here are some other titles in the series which you might like to read.

Sparrow
Veronica Heley
After her mother's death in an accident Vivien goes to live with her father and his noisy, untidy second family. She is desperately unhappy there and in her new school, a large comprehensive. Worst of all, she cannot go on with her piano and oboe lessons. In her loneliness and despair she remembers that God cares even for sparrows. She begins to see things in a new light and surprising openings appear for her musical talent.

The Eye of Time and Space
Dorothy Webb
Christine meets a mysterious stranger who gives her a box through which she can see into the past. She sees how God's plan has often involved suffering and learns how to handle her own unhappiness at school.

Code Red on Starship Englisia
Mark A. Durstewitz
During a space flight, Howard has to go outside the space ship to repair it. The control system on his spacesuit malfunctions and he almost loses his life but is saved by a strange light. What or who was the light? Howard's efforts to find out lead to more sinister dangers . . .

Left to Right
Eileen Taylor

Paul's hobby is running and he dreams of being famous one day. But when his mother walks out, his father goes into hospital and he is sent to stay with the family of a classmate whom he dislikes, he feels more like running away. Surprises are in store.